**FIN**

R. SAINT CLAIRE

Copyright © 2024 by R. Saint Claire

All rights reserved.

No part of this book may be reproduced in any form or by any electronic or mechanical means, including information storage and retrieval systems, without written permission from the author, except for the use of brief quotations in a book review.

Book cover design by Beetiful Book Covers

Editing by Andrew Lyall

*For my cherished theater family, especially those who get the inside jokes.*

# CHAPTER 1
TULLYTOWN PLAYERS 2003

The pages from the script trembled in her hand as if someone had turned on the wind-machine backstage. The theater was eerily quiet and, except for a rustling in the darkened house and the lights humming on the catwalk above, almost dead.

The downstage right wing, where she stood just behind the proscenium, cloaked her in comforting darkness; she could hide there, for now. She shifted the pages--theater people called them "sides"--from one sweaty hand to the next and tried mastering her breath. After all, her body was her instrument, and all great actors learned to play theirs like finely tuned harps, the best like a priceless Stradivarius. Of course, she wasn't on that level yet, but she'd learn. All she needed was that first big break.

She glanced down at her schoolgirl outfit wondering if it was a mistake, yanked the hem of the skirt to cover her thighs a bit. She wasn't trying to look sexy—although that couldn't hurt—but younger. Her audition piece was for a girl in her teens, and she had turned twenty-seven the previous week.

*But I still look young*, she thought hopefully, not quite convinced.

She knew she wasn't the prettiest girl in the world, but neither were her favorite stage actresses. Talent was what mattered.

Her nervousness was especially keen today because Dudley Wicks, *the* Dudley Wicks had just accepted the role of Tullytown Players artist in residence for the summer season. An acclaimed playwright and director by age thirty, Dudley Wicks had yet to shed his *wunderkind* crown. Not many artists could adapt a story about deaf mutes into a musical hit like he had with Carson McCullers' *The Heart is a Lonely Hunter*. Many doubted he could pull it off, but Wicks' creative instincts were infallible. The musical ran for four seasons on Broadway before continuing on a national tour to great acclaim. When a *Backstage* reporter had asked Wicks why he'd waste his time and talent on such a small-town theater like Tullytown Players, he answered that it was the only theater on the East Coast that took chances on new, experimental projects like his own.

Quickly refocusing her attention on the here and now, she gazed out on the empty stage lit by a single spot down center. It amazed her to think of what potential that space held when it was filled with actors, sets, costumes, brilliant words, conflict, drama--

"Next!" bellowed a deep bass voice from the dark house.

She froze.

"That's you," rasped the elderly stage manager, blending into the darkness in his *blacks*, the clothing all backstage personnel wore.

"Huh?" She was disoriented.

"You're on, kid." He gave her a gentle shove from behind.

She passed the thick velvet curtain, which draped each

side of the proscenium and stumbled over her penny loafers. Detecting a giggle from the house, she felt her face flush, but she recovered her composure and walked the width of *the boards* to the down center position.

*Find the light*, she reminded herself. When the heat of the Fresnel radiated on her cheeks, she gazed out into the house. Even in the cavernous darkness, she had no trouble locating Dudley Wicks in his white linen suit, a sartorial trademark the *Backstage* article described as affectatious. But artistic people, she reminded herself, were eccentric, while the rest of us struggling mortals were merely crazy.

*If only I can enter the realm of the artist, then I can truly be somebody.*

Richard "RJ" Jennings, the theater's artistic director extraordinaire, sat beside Wicks--a dream team if there ever was one. Fresh out of Yale's esteemed drama program, RJ had given up his Broadway career to convert an old barn into a thriving theater in a few short seasons. Handsome and somewhat stocky—although he appeared much taller on stage--RJ wore his black hair slicked back. The beard he'd grown while starring in the Chekhov production the previous season gave him an air of distinction.

"Hello. Who are you?" RJ boomed with his distinctive deep voice.

*Who? What?*

"Your name?"

Both men stared at her now.

The hot lights were making scrambled eggs of her brain.

Dudley Wicks leaned forward, indulgently draping his arms over the seat in front of him. An unlit cigarette dangled from his fingers. "You do have a name, don't you?"

The stage manager snickered from the wings.

"Y-yes. I'm sorry. My name is Candace Laherty."

"All right, Candace Laherty." RJ enunciated each syllable of her name, making it sound—dare she dream it?—like the name of a star.

RJ shifted through a stack of black and white headshots and resumes until he located hers. "Ah, here you are. What are you going to read for us today?"

"I'll be reading the part of Juliet from *Romeo and Juliet* before she kills herself."

Dudley Wicks settled back in his seat. "Interesting choice, and one so rarely seen."

*Was that sarcasm?*

Candace cast an anxious glance backstage. The stage manager made a twirling motion with his finger, signaling her to get on with it.

Candace opened her mouth, but the words she'd laboriously memorized died on her lips. She fumbled with the sides. The pages floated limply to her feet. She crouched to scoop them up and felt dizzy when she straightened.

When Juliet's speech finally spilled from Candace's mouth, the music of Shakespeare's words had been reduced to broken notes played on an out of tune fiddle, no Stradivarius.

"Thank you very much." RJ cut her off before she could withdraw the prop dagger from her skirt pocket and plunge it into her chest, a bit she'd been practicing in front of a mirror for days.

"But I'm not done," she pleaded.

"We know how it ends," droned Wicks.

RJ chuckled and said to Wicks, "Nice rack though."

*Is he talking about me?*

"May I please start again?" she asked, trembling, near tears.

*Final Dress* 5

"Sorry, but we have many actors to audition today," rejoined RJ, a ring of finality in his expressive voice.

Candace's cheeks reddened beneath the spotlight's glare.

"Can't you give me another chance?" Her shrill voice added another crack to the old barn's ceiling.

But RJ and Dudley were already shuffling through the stack of headshots and resumes, putting hers, no doubt, in the reject pile.

∽

DEPRESSED AND HUMILIATED, Candace remained in her car for most of the afternoon. Parked in the shade of the willow tree, she watched, with deepening envy, as her rival actors exited through the stage door. Some looked disappointed, but a few regulars bounced out excitedly gripping newly-printed scripts. She recognized voluptuous Liz Jennings, RJ's wife, smiling triumphantly, her raven hair swinging in the golden sunlight.

*It's not fair*, Candace thought bitterly. *The audition process is just for show. It's always rigged, and the only way to get ahead is to fuck the director!*

Candace sank down in the driver's seat when she saw RJ and Wicks emerge. They appeared happy, engaged, chatting intensely about the play no doubt. Candace imagined them heading to The General Greene Inn, the theater folks' local hangout. Over drinks, they'd excitedly discuss the play, the cast, and their plans to mount the production.

*And I'll be forgotten.*

Candace's heart sank like an anvil in quicksand. She was about to call it a day and head home, when she noticed the backdoor to the theater, the ones the stagehands used to load scenery, had been propped open. The stage manager, always the last to leave, must have neglected to check it.

Despite knowing it was a stupid venture, she felt compelled to return to the stage, to prove she had talent, if only to satisfy her own ego. She left her dented green Camry with the bad muffler and squeezed through the backdoor to enter a labyrinth of hallways, stairwells, ladders, and dark storage rooms.

Because the theater had once been a barn, it still smelled vaguely of hay and manure. She breathed the air deeply, loving it as much as the smell of the greasepaint sticks in the Ben Nye makeup kit she had recently purchased. She'd hoped to use it when she finally got cast in a show, a Dudley Wicks production, no less!

*But I blew it.*

Her tiny spotlight of hope dimmed, and no stardust could make it flame again. Pushing thirty in a dead-end job, the married lover who told her it was over between them just last week because his wife was pregnant.

*It's been fun, honey, but I have ambitions in this town that don't include a mistress.*

One reason she wanted a part in the play, it just occurred to her, was to show *him* what he was missing out on when he dumped her, show this whole damn town that she was talented, beautiful, accomplished. A Winner!

*I'll show them all!*

She fumbled her way to the right wing and gazed out at the empty stage. She had stood at that very spot only hours before. But now, the only light on stage was the solitary ghost light, an old theatrical tradition to drive away vengeful spirits. Maybe that's why she choked during her audition. A vengeful spirit had gotten her, her lover's pregnant wife perhaps?

*Final Dress* 7

Head held high, she entered the stage confidently and stopped when she reached dead center. Lit only by the ghost light's soft glow, Candace took a moment to center herself, then she began her Juliet monologue again. But unlike her earlier failure, the Bard's words burst from her tongue like water from a virgin spring. Her voice was strong, connected to the emotions of a young girl preparing to end her life for love. When she finished her speech, she was weeping.

*I'll go home now,* she thought, *pop in a TV dinner, catch up on the Real Housewives, and...*

Out there, in the darkness, something stirred.

"Hello? Is anyone there?" Her voice echoed in the empty house, then faded to silence.

*Probably just a mouse,* she thought. *This old barn is full of them.*

Having just proved, if only to herself, that she was a fine actress, Candace performed a deep curtsey to the empty house. Then, with the comportment of a seasoned diva, she turned and strolled upstage. Parting the black curtain, she entered the backstage area once again. A red exit light was the only illumination in the darkness. Groping around half-blind, she fumbled on a metal ladder, painted black. She knew enough about the theater to know this ladder led to *the heavens*, the area above the stage where lights are hung and stage scenery is stored.

Acting on instinct--an actor's primary tool--she climbed, hand over hand, with the energy of renewed purpose.

When she reached the catwalk, she paused momentarily at the top to catch her breath and then traversed the grated metal walkway until she stood directly over center stage. Dizzy from the height, she reached out to steady herself. Her hand landed on one of the ropes attached to heavy sandbags. She gazed up to where ropes ran from the barn's high cathedral ceiling to the catwalk, some coiled on the floor like snakes. She didn't pretend to understand the complicated fly system of raising and lowering scenery, but the ropes could have another purpose.

Now, it all made sense to her why she'd made the climb.

One rope was attached to a large sandbag. Next to it was a piece of castle scenery from a production of *Camelot*. Of course, RJ had given the role of Guinevere to Liz, whose only talent was shoving her boobs in the leading man's face.

The double doors from the back of the house burst open, spilling in light from the lobby and lengthening the shadow of the lone figure entering the space.

A deep voice resonated. "Candace, I saw your car outside. Listen, we need to talk."

Candace knew that voice, knew the reason why he'd come. He was trying to control the situation, control her, keep her quiet.

*Well, he's about to see a performance he'll never forget.*

Candace looped the end of one rope around her neck and quickly fastened a tight knot against her throat.

Her breath quickened with a renewed sense of purpose. She could almost hear the orchestra warming up in the pit below. It was nearly time for her entrance.

"Candace!" the man called, walking down the center aisle toward the stage. "I know you're here."

After securing the rope, she straddled the railing of the catwalk, one leg then the other, so that she stood outside gripping the bars. She was nervous, terrified even, but that was natural before a big entrance--and opening night to boot! In her agitated state of mind, it seemed to her that the houselights dimmed. Even from this great a height, she could hear the audience buzzing with anticipation.

She looked down excitedly, her gaze landing on the red

cue light pulsing from the darkened left wing like a demon's eye. She waited for the light to cue her entrance, if only in her mind.

The red light blinked out.

"Watch me!" she shouted and stepped into the abyss. The sandbag, more than twice her weight, held firm against the catwalk railing; the rope caught, cutting off the involuntary scream rasping from her throat. Her shoes flew off and thudded to the boards. Her feet danced above the floor in a desperate reach.

She heard him shout, "Candace, no!" And with dimming eyesight watched as he scrambled onto the stage.

Then blackout!

## CHAPTER 2
TULLYTOWN PLAYERS 2024

Shawna gazed out of the passenger window of her Dad's black Lexus SUV at the beautiful green suburban landscape in an attempt to quell her excitement, along with a lingering unease. The following day marked the start of her new internship at the theater, which would be cause enough for jitters. But tonight was also the opening gala for the new season--a celebration of Tullytown Players' 30th anniversary, a remarkable milestone for the East Coast's most successful community theater. She hoped to make a good impression on Rick Jennings and the rest of the theater crew, to be someone they could rely upon throughout the summer season, not just tolerated because she was the Mayor's kid.

Shawna tugged on the hem of her cocktail dress, wondering if it was too revealing. The outfit was bought impulsively at the mall with $250 of her college graduation money. For someone barely five feet tall and weighing less than one hundred pounds, most fancy dresses made her look like a child. But her attempt at sophistication in a copy of Princess Diana's black *revenge dress* may have hideously backfired.

Her Dad, William Anthony the Third, whom everyone in town called Mayor Bill--the ones who liked him, that is--made a face she'd grown to know too well since her mom's untimely death. The look conveyed both pity and disapproval; Shawna hated both.

Bill's police radio buzzed beneath the dash.

"Does that thing need to be on?" Shawna asked.

He reached under the dash and dialed down the knob. "If there's an emergency tonight, they'll find me." He shot her a sidelong glance.

"What, Dad?"

"I don't know why you're so nervous."

"I'm not nervous, just shy around new people. Remember the psychology course I took?"

"Hmm."

"We all took personality tests, and I'm an INFP."

"What's that?"

"It stands for introverted, intuitive, feeling, and perceiving."

"Translation?"

"It means I'm an idealist."

"Ah! You needed a Bryn Mawr degree to tell you that."

Shawna smiled. "Whatever, Dad."

Bill leaned into the rearview mirror to check his teeth for any remnants of their Applebee's dinner. "I'm the one who should be nervous. Why did I ever agree to give a speech?" He sighed as if it were the last thing he wanted to do. "Is the--"

"Is the thing still in the backseat?" Shawna turned to make sure. "For the hundredth time, yes. It's still there."

Under Bill's leadership, the town celebrated the theater's achievement by commissioning two bronze-tone comedy and tragedy masks. Accompanying the masks was a framed certificate signed by the city council members.

Shawna flipped down the lighted mirror to apply peachy lip gloss as they neared the theater.

"Hey, go easy on the greasepaint. Your mom and I raised you to use your brains."

Shawna rolled her eyes.

"I still don't understand why you chose to intern at Tullytown Players. I mean, isn't the-a-ter--" he pronounced each syllable with affected flair, "--rendered obsolete by the invention of film, television, TikTok videos?"

"Of course not. People will always appreciate live theater."

"Are you sure about that?"

"Media Studies happened to be my minor, Dad."

"Don't remind me."

She playfully slapped his thigh.

"Couldn't you do an internship where you could learn something useful?"

"Useful like..."

"Business, politics, law, real estate."

Now it was her turn to make a face.

"Speaking of real estate, I still think all this farmland would be better suited for--"

"I know, Dad, a housing project."

"Do you know the theater rents all thirty acres of this beautiful farmland for one dollar a year?"

"Yes, you told me. The town gave them a hundred-year lease on it, too."

The car bumped along the gravel driveway when they entered the theater parking lot.

"Look at the bright side, Dad," chirped Shawna.

Bill rubbed his freshly shaved chin. "What's that?"

"You only have to wait seventy years."

"Very funny. At least they could fix up this place." Bill glanced at the converted barn's sagging roof. "When was the last time anyone painted it?"

"Why doesn't the town pay for it?"

"Are you serious?" Bill looked aghast. "We've already poured a fortune into this white elephant."

"Well," Shawna said with a flutter of excitement. "Maybe I can start a fundraising project."

He turned to his daughter and smiled. Despite his grumblings, he was damn proud of her and how much she looked like her mother in that fancy dress. His eyes misted.

"What, Dad?"

"Nothing."

Bill pulled into the last available parking space beneath a willow tree's bowing branches.

"Looks like quite a crowd tonight." His voice lacked enthusiasm.

Shawna's mood was the opposite. Her heart beat excitedly as she gazed at the enormous barn with its faded red paint. The words Tullytown Players, writ large on its front face in bold white letters, looked as dazzling to her as any Broadway marquee.

Bill opened the door for Shawna. She climbed out of the vehicle, brushing the bright red curls she inherited from her Dad over one shoulder.

"Madame," Bill said, proffering his arm. They strolled toward the entrance, where loud, happy chatter drifted through the open sliding barn door.

"Oh wait!" Shawna said. "The masks!"

Bill sighed. "How could I forget? Those damn masks cost

as much as your tuition last year. Don't forget the certificate too."

"Got it." Dashing back to the car to retrieve them, her stomach swirled with nerves and excitement.

As soon as they entered the lobby, converted for the evening into a ballroom, Bill handed the shopping bag containing the masks and certificates to one of the gala volunteers, instructing her to stash it beneath the podium for when he gave his speech later. They spotted Rick Jennings threading, a bit unsteadily, through the crowd toward them.

"Someone's already in his cups," muttered Bill before Shawna could land a sharp elbow to his ribs.

"Mayor Bill!" RJ's baritone thundered.

"RJ!" Bill said with his best politician's grin.

Bypassing Bill's extended hand, RJ wrapped Bill in a bear hug. Shawna suppressed a giggle at her Dad's chagrin.

*Theater people.*

Shawna noted how fit and trim RJ appeared in his tuxedo. If it weren't for the white streaks in his black hair and beard, he'd have passed for a man ten years his junior. RJ was a well-known figure around town, with a bit of a reputation. Shawna had heard about his infamous drunken episode at The General Greene Inn a year ago where he performed scenes from *The Iceman Cometh* until the police had to be called. Bill made sure the papers kept it quiet, but local tongues wagged. Still, after a brief stint *out of town*, RJ proved his physical prowess when he returned to tread the boards the previous season with his acclaimed portrayal of Sir Thomas More in *A Man For All Seasons*. Seeing that play turned Shawna into a fan. In Shawna's mind, Richard Jennings may be old, but he was a star.

RJ swung his gaze toward Shawna. "And who is this lovely young lady?"

Shawna squirmed with embarrassment when RJ's eyes dropped from her face to her chest and remained locked there.

"This is my daughter, Shawna. She's going to be your intern for the season."

RJ's grin widened, and his warm brown eyes twinkled. Shawna decided there and then that RJ had charm, something she, as a shy introvert, lacked.

"Oh, that's right," RJ said. "My wife told me. I never expected someone so lovely." He smoothly lifted Shawna's hand to his lips in a gesture worthy of Don Juan. Shawna's intense embarrassment was saved by Liz Jennings, RJ's wife, crashing into them from behind.

"RJ," she whined, not noticing or caring that wine splashed on her sleeve from the glass she held. "There's a couple you got to meet. Sheldon Scrimshaw and his wife are here, the ones with the big bucks." She rubbed her fingers together.

Shawna quickly took in Liz's appearance. The yellowing lobby posters depicted a much younger version of Tullytown Players' resident *grande dame*. Her unnaturally black hair made her rouged cheeks appear garish beneath the lights of the lobby chandeliers. Her flowing outfit did little to hide the hundred-odd pounds she'd gained since her debut as Luisa in *The Fantasticks*.

"Liz, darling," RJ said, coloring slightly at his wife's faux pas. "Mayor Bill and his daughter are here."

Liz clutched her chest dramatically, spilling more wine on herself. "I'm so sorry; I didn't notice you standing there."

After a brief and effusive greeting, Liz excused herself to pursue a tray of hors-d'oeuvres.

Shawna was working up the courage to compliment RJ on his latest performance when a woman stepped up and dragged him away. Shawna recognized the toothsome blonde as Penny McNeil, who had played the female lead in *Footloose* the previous season. Although she would never voice it, Shawna found most of Penn's performances weak and often wondered why RJ continued to cast her.

Shawna tracked them across the lobby, where they joined Hutch Davidson, Tullytown Players' handsome leading man, and a tall black man wearing a gold dinner jacket accented with a matching bowler hat.

"That must be Rex Fawn, the New York choreographer," Shawna said to her Dad. She watched RJ lean in and whisper something that caused the group to explode with laughter.

Shawna observed, with some discomfort, that Tullytown Players was a tight clique, like those mean girls at her school who ignored anyone who didn't want to join a sorority. Shawna wished she had made more friends at college. Her bestie, Terry, was spending a year abroad studying medieval art in Italy.

*But maybe*, she thought while surveying the exuberant crowd, *I'll make new friends here.*

"Excuse me, Mayor." A shrill voice contrasted with the theatrical chatter around them. Bill spun and immediately blanched at the sight of Dale Cartwright. Dale, a recent NYC School of Journalism graduate, took her reporting job at the Tullytown Times much too seriously for most of the town's old guard.

With her faded jeans and nose ring, Dale looked out of place at the formal event. Bill attempted to hide his disdain behind a pasted-on smile.

"Ah, hello, Dale," Bill said. "Enjoying the festivities?"

Dale brushed her lanky brown bangs from her eyes. "Mayor, I'm here on official business."

Bill blinked. "Oh?"

"Do you have a statement to make about the new information over the disappearance of Candace Laherty?"

Dale's assertive, some might say aggressive tone caught the attention of a few revelers.

"Candace Laherty?" Bill repeated slowly.

"Let me refresh your memory, Mayor. She was a local woman who went missing over twenty years ago."

"And?"

"Her car was discovered in Neshaminy Creek this morning, the section that cuts through Reynold's farmland. It may never have been discovered if it weren't for some local kids climbing the fence to hunt for crayfish."

"Ah, yes." Bill's naturally ruddy face turned a deeper shade of red. He took Dale's arm and steered her toward the exit. Shawna followed, eavesdropping on the conversation.

Bill lowered his voice and said, "The police department will address it first thing tomorrow morning at the press conference. I'll be there, too."

Dale shrugged off Bill's touch as if it were patriarchal poison.

"Yeah," said Dale. "I got that. I wanted to know if you have any particular statement, or..." she looked past him, "perhaps I'll start asking around. After all, Candace Laherty's last known whereabouts was this theater."

Bill was struggling to respond when RJ arrived like the cavalry in time to rescue the Mayor from the strident young journalist's assault.

"Ms. Cartwright," RJ interrupted with a voice smooth as silk, "It's lovely to see you again."

"Don't mean to crash your party," Dale said, her hard

shell melting somewhat in the vapor of RJ's charm, "but I'm covering the disappearance of Candace Laherty and--"

"Ah," RJ steepled his fingers beneath his beard. "Terrible news about the car. We were hoping," he shrugged theatrically, "that she was off living her life, happy somewhere. Candace was a treasured member of our community. If we can assist in any way, please don't hesitate to ask."

Appearing self-conscious, Dale slid her notebook into the back pocket of her jeans.

"Will you stay and have a drink with us?" RJ gestured expansively toward the crowded bar.

"Uh. No thanks." Her gaze slid back to Bill and hardened. "I'll save the rest of my questions for the press conference. Goodnight."

RJ bowed slightly. "Goodnight, my dear."

Both men stood side by side and watched her leave.

"I've seen better asses in my day, but not many," RJ said, breaking the tension.

Bill threw his head back, laughed, and polished off his watered-down bourbon.

RJ turned to Shawna, "I apologize for my crassness."

Shawna said, "That's okay," and giggled uncomfortably, wondering how that exchange would be received by her Women's Study Seminar.

RJ took hold of Bill's glass. "Let's freshen that drink for you."

"Hey, watch where you're going!"

RJ nearly toppled over a woman in a wheelchair. Shawna observed the elderly woman's silver hair styled in an elegant upsweep and decided there was something regal about her appearance. Her purple pleated gown was simple yet majestic. Oversized spectacles adorned with rhinestones obscured her handsome face.

RJ bent down to kiss the woman's cheek, then turned to his guests and said, "Bill, Shawna, meet Harriet Harman, our bookkeeper. Without her, we'd be lost."

Harriet smiled up at RJ. "Well, that's true. Pleased to meet you, Shawna." Her dark, intense gaze shifted from Shawna to Bill. "Your father and I have met before."

"Of course. Wonderful to see you again," Bill replied smoothly, although it was obvious he had no idea who she was. Shawna pitied her Dad at that moment. Meeting so many people and trying to remember their names must be difficult.

"Harriet practically lives here," RJ boomed. "She's the only reason we can keep the lights on." RJ swung his gaze at Shawna. "If you have any questions about the ins and outs of this place, Harriet's your gal."

"Thank you," Shawna replied shyly. "I'll try to remember that." From the corner of her eye, she saw that Hutch was standing alone by the concession stand. Here was her chance to have a conversation with the leading man.

Shawna excused herself and made a hesitant beeline toward Hutch.

She felt self-conscious and mousy when she shyly approached him. "Excuse me, but I just wanted to tell you how much I loved your performance in *Footloose*." She didn't mention how he was far too old to play the role of a rebellious dancing teenager.

Her self-consciousness melted when Hutch beamed at the praise. "Well, thank you very much. That's so sweet of you."

Before Shawna could tell him he sang better than the actor in the Broadway production, Penny slid in next to Hutch, flipped her blond locks over one shoulder, and sucked on the straw of her Piña Colada. Her heavily mascaraed eyes narrowed at Shawna.

"Penny was great playing Ariel," Hutch said.

"Of course," Shawna said. "You were both great."

Shawna found it difficult to lie.

"Thanks," Penny said flatly. "What's brings you to the gala?"

"Well," Shawna said. "The Mayor is my dad."

Penny raised an eyebrow. "Really?" She appeared about to say something else, when she became distracted.

"Oh, my God!" Penny set down her drink and rushed past Shawna, knocking into her slightly. "Dudley Wicks is here!"

Hutch apologized on Penny's behalf and thanked Shawna again for the praise before rushing off to press the flesh with the Broadway legend. Wicks was returning to Tullytown Players to mount the premiere of his new play as part of the milestone anniversary season. The local newspaper articles made it seem like a big deal, but secretly, Shawna wondered if Dudley Wicks could even produce a new show on Broadway or Off-Broadway for that matter. He last few attempts were flops.

Still, Dudley Wicks maintained a certain level of charisma in his signature white linen suit. Despite now sporting a full head of white hair, the former wunderkind hadn't aged much. He still maintained the same svelte physique of an artist who survives on coffee, cigarettes, and perhaps other stimulants. Wicks took a moment to shake hands and work the room before RJ handed him a drink. Liz rammed her way to the front of the pack to fold Wicks in a motherly embrace. Rex raised a glass to toast the renowned playwright. The room swelled with new energy. Shawna felt it too, like lightning bolts through her skin.

She just knew this would be a summer she'd never forget!

**CHAPTER 3**

The Tullytown Times ran a photo of Mayor Bill handing RJ the award. Shawna thought Bill's serious expression and RJ's wide grin perfectly mirrored the comedy/tragedy masks. Bill complained he looked "jowly" in the photo and vowed to burn more calories on the golf course this summer. Unlike her Dad, Shawna could eat ice cream every night and never gain an ounce, but the morning she was to start her internship, she was too excited to eat. If she doubted her decision to intern at the theater, the gala had sealed the deal for her.

*Guess I've caught the theater bug*, she thought as she happily pedaled her bicycle the short mile and a half from her upscale neighborhood, Pennbrook Farms, to the old Reynold's farmland that felt like entering a pastoral world of centuries past.

Shawna could tell that Blake, the stage manager, wasn't a morning person by her response, or rather lack of response, to Shawna's cheerful good morning. But it didn't curtail the young intern's enthusiasm. Shawna had spotted Blake mixing drinks behind the bar at the gala wearing her theater "blacks" and a bow tie and guessed Blake was one of the few staff members on salary. Volunteers mostly ran the old barn, filling in the box office and usher positions. Temporary backstage crews were hired according to each production's needs. The actors received a small stipend if Non-equity and the lowest end of Actors' Equity pay scale if they had their prized "card." The amateur/professional hybrid status of Tullytown Players made it unique and a step above standard community theaters.

Blake had a no-nonsense air about her. She looked to be around thirty with a crop of short brown hair tucked beneath a trucker hat and a pale, makeup-less complexion. Between grumpy gulps of a 20 oz. coffee, Blake instructed Shawna to set out water glasses, yellow notepads, and sharpened pencils before each place at the long table running the length of the stage. First rehearsals always began with a meet and greet followed by a table read of the script. Shawna took her assignment seriously, ensuring each notepad and pencil was placed neatly and at right angles. She took extra care filling Hutch's water glass, careful not to spill a drop.

At nine am, Blake eyed her watch with an Eeyore sigh and announced, "It's showtime, folks."

Shawna's heart beat wildly when the double doors in the back of the house burst open, and the cast, director, and designers filed in. Even though they had just been partying together the night before, they greeted each other as if reunited after long sea journeys.

Looking fresh in a blue linen blazer, RJ made his way onto the stage, followed by Liz, who wore a velvet mauve tracksuit that had seen better days. Spontaneous applause erupted as RJ mounted "the boards." Liz beamed behind RJ as he strolled downstage to take a bow. Shawna assumed this was some theatrical tradition of which, she guessed, there were many. With a flush of self-consciousness, she realized she had much to learn.

"So, we didn't scare you away the other night, eh?"

Shawna turned and blinked in the bright beam of Hutch's smile. Hutch looked like one of the underwear models from the old *International Male* catalogs she'd clipped images from for a project in her Gender Studies class. She couldn't help but imagine what Hutch looked like in an open necked pirate shirt and a leopard print thong.

"Hi, Sara." Penny waved in Shawna's direction. "Nice to see you again."

"It's Shawna," Shawna said with a friendly smile. "Nice to see you too."

Unlike Hutch, Penny did not appear as fresh under the glare of the harsh work lights. Shawna wondered how long Penny could continue playing the ingenue roles.

"Oh," Penny snapped her fingers. "Shawna. Sorry, it's such a whirlwind." She made a twirling gesture with her lacquered nails to illustrate her point. "Well, welcome aboard, and keep those water glasses filled." Her fingers fluttered over her throat. "The voice, you know. Come on, babe." Penny's hand formed a claw around Hutch's muscled bicep as she yanked him away.

Shawna turned to see if Blake needed any help. Everyone had already found their seats at the table, and a hush had fallen over the company. Shawna took her place off to the side. Blake told her that her role would be to assist anyone needing missing Xeroxes or sharpened pencils. A good soldier in any situation, Shawna was armed, ready for battle, and very excited, albeit a bit nervous.

Dudley Wicks was the last to arrive, entering furtively stage left in his white suit, and creeping toward the last empty seat at the table. But he was intersected by RJ, who welcomed him with a prolonged bear hug. At the same time, a beaming Liz girlishly clapped her hands, igniting a raucous round of applause from the entire company for the Broadway professional in their midst. Wicks made a humble bow and took his seat.

Although Shawna clapped along with the rest of the company, she sensed some grandiosity in Wicks' reserved appearance. She thought he'd at least give a short speech about the play, considering the production they were about to mount was the official out-of-town tryout. She wondered, with a pang, if Wicks considered Tullytown Players beneath him.

As the reading began and the cast settled in, Shawna decided that Wick's attitude was probably just insecurity brought about by all his Broadway flops. People often overcompensate for insecurity by showing disdain.

She had learned a lot in her second-semester Psych class.

## CHAPTER 4

The read-thru lasted most of the morning, and Shawna wondered if she was the only one who needed help following the script. She'd even caught herself nodding off a few times. The play, a musical adaptation of the classic Greek tragedy *Agamemnon*, seemed a convoluted concept at best. Despite a few catchy songs, the story felt disjointed to Shawna, who was fresh from a Bryn Mawr classic drama seminar. But she quickly reminded herself that play readings were often dull. The story would come alive during the rehearsal process, which was set to start the following day. As a treat for the season's first day, the theatre provided sandwiches and salads for everyone. Shawna felt somewhat embarrassed when she caught Liz in the dressing room front-loading a slice of pepperoni pizza.

"Non-gluten," Liz said, looking sheepish.

Shawna had entered the women's dressing room with an armload of costumes as per Blake's instructions.

"Oh, I'm sorry. I should have knocked, but-"

"It's no problem." Liz wiped the grease from her chin

with a paper napkin. "It's nice to have you here." Her heavily lined eyes twinkled. "So, what do you think of the play?"

Shawna plopped the heavy costumes in the nearest chair.

"Well, I think it's very interesting," Shawna answered in what she considered a *safe* response.

"Interesting!" Liz's eyes rolled to the ceiling. "It's genius!"

Liz had been cast in the female lead role of Clytemnestra, the vengeful queen who murders her husband Agamemnon along with the young Trojan Princess Cassandra, whom he made into his concubine as a spoil of war. Hutch and Penny were to play the roles of Agamemnon and Cassandra.

"Dudley Wicks is *the* only talent out of New York right now--the only one worth anything. Back when I was on Broadway--"

Dudley Wick's frame filled the threshold, cutting off Liz's words with a clearing of his throat. His white linen suit showed some creases from sitting at the read-through all morning.

"Oh! I was just singing your praises," gushed Liz. "I was telling Sally here--"

"Shawna."

"Lizzie darling," Wicks interrupted. His tanned face showed all the downward stress of intense annoyance. "Something needs to be done about the artist's residence. I was late this morning because there are mice in the kitchen."

Liz swiped the pizza crust crumbs from her velour onto the floor. "I'm so sorry. I will speak with Ron immediately about it."

Just then, a short, heavy-set woman tottered into the dressing room with only the top half of her face visible over an armload of costumes. She squeezed past Wicks with a groan.

"Well, that's most of the classical stuff. Where do you want these, Mrs. J?"

"Oh, Judith, just drop them anywhere."

Wicks rolled his eyes to the ceiling. "Oh, never mind. I'll speak to Ron myself." He turned and left in a huff.

"Dudley, wait!" Liz shuffled out of her chair and pursued Wick into the hall.

Judith, a squat middle-aged woman who had probably looked the same since her twenties, dumped the load of costumes on top of the ones Shawna brought in and then flopped into the empty chair next to it. Pressing a hand over her beating heart, she closed her eyes tightly.

"Are you okay?" asked Shawna. She worried Judith was having a heart attack, but then again, everyone at the theater seemed to have a dramatic flair about them. But the wardrobe lady, too?

Judith shushed her, then pressed two fingers into the side of her throat. "Just counting my pulse. Give me a minute."

Shawna's eyes flew to the clock on the wall. Judith took thirty seconds to time her pulse before expelling a huff of breath. "All right." Judith pointed at an empty rolling rack against the wall. "Hang this stuff up before it gets wrinkled. That steamer of ours isn't the best. I asked Ron for a new one. What? Last year?"

"Who's Ron?" Shawna asked. She wanted to make sure she knew everyone's name.

"You work at this theater and you don't know who Ron is?" Judith glanced in one the lighted makeup mirrors and fluffed her black bowl haircut. "Boy, they don't break you kids in like they did in the old days, do they? This place is too cheap to build me a proper wardrobe room. How many years have I been asking Ron to fix that? Too many. That's how many. So, we're stuck working in here. Seen my scissors anywhere? Ah, there they are. If you lose 'em, you pay for 'em, and they weren't cheap. Got it?"

"Uh—"

"Good."

Still not having learned the identity of the elusive Ron and afraid to ask because of how Judith might respond, Shawna quickly got down to work, placing each costume on a hanger and then arranging them in a neat row on a rolling rack. She noticed, with concern, that most of the costumes were stiff with age, some even torn and stained.

When a cloud of dust erupted from one costume Shawna sneezed and quickly apologized. "I think I'm allergic to mold."

"Tell me about it," Judith replied. "This barn is a petri dish of infection and a minefield for other things." She narrowed her eyes behind her thick, rectangular eyeglasses. "And never forget, the walls have ears."

"What do you mean?"

Judith glanced at the open dressing room door, alerting to any lingering minions. "Have you met Dougal?"

"Dougal?"

"Dougal," Judith said impatiently. "The TD."

"TD?"

"The Technical Director. Don't they teach you college kids nothing no more?" Judith shook her head, the shadow of a mustache visible over her tightened lips.

"Oh, right." Shawna had seen a shady-looking dude in an ill-fitting suit smoking a cigarette outside the theater when she and her Dad left the gala. She recalled her Dad mumbling about being on her guard around the techies. "No, I haven't officially met him yet."

"Well, watch out for him and Ron. Word on the street is they're using the theater as their personal pharmacy, and Harriet is covering it up. There's something shady about her too. But you didn't hear that from me." Judith mimed locking her lips closed and tossing away the key.

Shawna thought she'd probably never met anyone as pleasant and harmless as Harriet and dismissed Judith's rants as silly gossip.

"These tunics are nice, though," Shawna said, wading into safer conversational waters. "Did you make all of these?"

"Built."

"Huh?"

"In the theater, costumes are built, not made."

"Oh, right."

"I'd have to be as old as Methuselah to have built those costumes. Look at the labels."

Shawna peeled back the neckline of one of the less moldy tunics to inspect a faded label sewn into the seam. "Does that say The Majestic Theater on Broadway?"

"Uh-huh. These were from the original production of *Forum* in 1962."

"Really? But isn't *Forum* set in Roman Times? I thought this production was set in Ancient Greece."

Judith glared at Shawna over her eyeglasses. "Listen, smarty pants. There ain't much difference between a toga and a tunic, okay?"

"Oh, sure. I didn't mean to offend you."

"One of those costumes had Zero Mostel's name on it. I'm pretty sure a former intern stole it." Judith eyed Shawna suspiciously.

"Oh, I wouldn't do that."

"Let's hope not. Anyway. We received a lot of old Broadway cast-offs over the years. These could be in better shape, but who has time to build new ones? Know how to sew?"

"Uh, no. Sorry."

Judith shook her head sadly. "See? They don't teach young girls anything anymore. I always say once they got rid of the Home Ec. classes--"

"I'd love to learn how to sew!"

"You think I have time to teach you? You think they pay me to do that?"

"Oh, I just thought--"

"Yeah. Everyone around here thinks too much. That's what I think. Well," Judith groaned as she hoisted herself from the chair. "You steam those, and I'll try to round up some better ones. There's probably more costumes in the hayloft storage, but they don't pay me enough to go up there."

Shawna was about to offer to do whatever Judith needed, but the wardrobe lady was already out the door, grumbling how no one appreciates her.

Deciding that Judith was just another one of Tullytown Players' theatrical characters to add to the list, Shawna got down to work. She dutifully steamed and pressed costumes for most of the afternoon, longing to return to the stage where the real magic was happening.

# CHAPTER 5

Rex Fawn stood down stage right observing the small chorus of dancers like a farmer inspecting cattle. The choreographer's hair was freshly faded; his cropped t-shirt showcased his impressive physique honed by years of dancing on Broadway stages and touring companies. And now, as Rex was approaching forty, he wanted to give back to the small theater where he'd gotten his start, at least that's what the arts section of The Tullytown Times had asserted.

Rex clapped his large hands together, and shouted, "Five, six, seven, eight!"

Blake cued the musical track, and the chorus, a mixed bag of local amateurs, including one retiree, two teenage girls with some dance training, and an awkward teenage boy without any coordination at all, began to mark the dance number Rex had just taught them. These were the Non-Equity actors, volunteers without nine-to-five jobs. Shawna recognized one of the dancers, a stunning brunette named Katie with swinging braids who worked part-time at the local dance store where Shawna had purchased a black leotard and tights for her college's Performance Art Seminar.

Enthralled by the performers on stage, Shawna yearned for their self-assurance. Becoming an actress may have seemed out of reach, but it was a cherished aspiration. Shawna's Dad, overhearing her belting out show tunes in the shower and singing along to the radio on long drives, remarked many times on her singing talent, but Shawna lacked confidence, that ability to stand on a stage like she belonged there. She also had a natural gift for dance, but alas no formal training. She regretted now signing up for the Reading Olympics rather than Jazz and Tap classes. And now, standing so close to a talented artist like Rex Fawn, she couldn't help but wonder if she, too, could one day grace the stage as a performer instead of just assisting backstage. Was she already succumbing to showbiz allure?

Shawna was about to shove those dreams back to her subconscious where they belonged and return to the dressing room for more costume drudgery when Rex signaled Hutch and Penny to enter the dance from stage left. Penny's rehearsal outfit consisted of black character shoes worn with a purple terrycloth romper barely covering her butt cheeks. But despite her slim figure, Shawna observed her bad posture and how much she struggled to keep up with Rex's choreography.

"Nope. Wrong," Rex stopped the movement with a loud clap. He pointed at Penny's feet. "You're turning out on that last combination."

"But you said pirouette." Penny's voice was annoying and whiny, chafing on Shawna's nerves.

"It's a jazz pirouette," countered Rex, his clipped tone indicating he had no time for whiners. "Like this." Rex demonstrated the move perfectly.

Penny glanced at Hutch for support, but the tall leading man was focused on perfecting his own moves. Penny looked away, frustrated.

"All right, let's try it again," called Rex. "Find your spots-- a-a-n-d--five, six, seven, eight!"

Catching herself gazing intently at Hutch from the upstage right wing, Shawna was aware of her raging hormones. She'd never had a boyfriend, never took boys seriously. She was probably the only virgin left in her entire graduating class. She'd often wondered if she was gender-neutral as some of her classmates claimed to be. Or maybe, she considered while she focused her gaze on Hutch's glistening thighs as he moved through the routine, she was never interested in boys, or girls for that matter. Only men!

"Excuse me," gruffed a voice behind her.

Shawna whirled out of her sensual musings to see Judith wearing a sour expression that perfectly mirrored the grumpy cat design on her printed t-shirt.

"Oh, I'm sorry, Judith. Do you need me for something?"

"You're supposed to be steaming those costumes. Remember?"

"I'm so sorry. I forgot. I guess I got, uh, distracted."

Judith's gaze clouded as she watched Hutch gyrate his hips to the musical beat. The movement accentuated the enormous bulge in his Lycra shorts.

"He's terrific, isn't he?" Shawna said in a quiet voice.

"He's not just good," Judith answered breathlessly, "he's mesmerizing."

"So, about those costumes," Shawna said with a laugh.

"Oh, right." Judith gripped Shawna's arm and pulled her backstage. "Let's go."

Once they were safely out of performers' earshot, Judith said, "If you want my opinion, that Penny isn't a patch on

Hutch's ass. But RJ keeps casting her year after year. I guess we know why." Judith flung open the women's dressing room. "Okay, get started on that rack."

Shawna's heart sank when she saw the rack so packed with costumes that the metal bar drooped as if about to snap. "We're using all of those?"

"No, we're not using all of those." Judith rudely mocked Shawna's voice.

"Then why do I have to steam all of them?" Shawna replied, a bit of Bryn Mawr snobbishness coloring her tone.

"Because, genius," snapped Judith. "We need them to look good for the fittings."

Shawna forcefully suppressed the urge to snap back. It was clear that Judith was what her Psych 101 course referred to as a "challenging personality." Shawna recalled her father's advice about the importance of diplomacy, especially in local politics. *Build bridges, not enemies*, was his motto. However, he also emphasized the need to stand up for oneself and not tolerate any nonsense.

Shawna cleared her throat. "You seem a little out of sorts today, Judith. Did you get enough sleep last night?"

"Sleep!" Judith huffed. "What's that?"

"Never mind," Shawna said and bent down to flip the switch on the steamer.

"Don't forget fittings are after lunch."

"Okay," Shawna said, relieved to see Judith heading for the door.

Prepping costumes for several hours was a tedious chore. Shawna singed herself twice on the hot steam. She was starting to think her Dad might have been right about this internship when Judith burst into the dressing room and breathlessly asked, "Have you seen Blake?"

"No, why?"

"There was an accident on stage."

Shawna quickly turned off the machine and trailed Judith to the stage, where the entire cast and crew were clustered around Penny, who sat on the stage floor, white as a sheet. RJ stood over her, and Hutch squatted beside her. Both men looked concerned.

Blake strolled in from stage left carrying a first aid kit and barked, "Alright, coming through."

While everyone was focused on Penny, Shawna noticed Wicks and Rex with heads bent together chatting near the stage right proscenium. Shawna took a few furtive steps toward them and stood behind one of the black masking curtains to listen in on their conversation.

"She can't keep up with the routine," Rex explained. "I tried to simplify the moves, but--"

"I've never thought she was right for Cassandra," added Wicks. "That should go to a girl of twenty at the oldest, not thirty-six. And the way she smokes and drinks, no wonder she can't keep up."

"She just not right for the part," said Rex, a bit more kindly.

"I'll speak to RJ about it."

Rex laughed. "Good luck. She's his favorite, and we all know why."

Wicks turned and noticed Shawna standing there.

"Oh, I'm sorry," she said, backing away into the wings, hoping to vanish.

"Wait just one moment," Wicks said.

Shawna braced for a verbal tearing down. It was apparent she was eavesdropping.

"I-I wasn't listening, I swear."

Wick silenced her with an upraised palm. "Are you in

the cast?" His eyes scanned her up and down before settling on her face.

Now Rex was observing her, too.

"No, I-I'm the intern. My name's Shawna Anthony." She was introduced to everyone at the first meeting, but with everything going on, why would they remember?

"Are you in high school?" Wicks asked sharply. Shawna noticed the unlit cigarette held between the fingers of his right hand, wondering if this too, along with his perennial white suit, was an affectation.

"Uh, no. I just graduated from college."

"Where?"

"Brynn Mar."

"Ah." Wicks glanced at Rex and raised an eyebrow. "Ms. Hepburn's alma mater. Impressive. Smart as well as cute."

Shawna blushed at the unexpected praise, but also inside, her heart sang.

Back at Shawna, Wicks asked, "How would you like to understudy the role of Cassandra?"

His words sucked the breath from Shawna's lungs. She could barely speak. "Are you serious? Me understudy for Cassandra?"

Penny rose like Lazarus from her fainting spell. Using both Hutch and RJ as crutches, she hobbled over to Wicks and Rex. The color had returned to her face, which was now flushed pink.

"I don't need an understudy," Penny said, her eyes shooting daggers at Shawna.

"If you are going to pass out during rehearsal, then I'm sorry, darling, but you do need an understudy," Wicks stated with authority. "Besides, it's standard procedure in any professional theater."

"I just got a little dizzy," Penny said. "I'm perfectly fine."

Wicks swung a questioning gaze at RJ.

RJ placed a fatherly hand on Penny's shoulder. "It's a good idea for Shawna to understudy all the female parts. It's what professional theaters do; we always try to be professional."

Biting her lip, Penny whirled on Shawna. "Fine. But you'll be wasting your time. I don't intend to miss one performance." With that, Penny stomped off. RJ trailed after her, to soothe her feelings, Shawna hoped.

"What a miraculous recovery," Wicks quipped to Rex, who burst out laughing.

Blake interrupted with an announcement. "Whoever keeps removing the paint can that holds open the back door, cut it out. We still haven't found the key, and I don't want to get locked out--again!"

"Everyone copy that?" bellowed RJ, who had returned to the stage looking annoyed. Perhaps his tête-à-tête with Penny hadn't gone so well.

A chorus of yesses followed.

"Alright. Five minutes," said Blake, and headed for the backstage door with a cigarette ready to fire.

A few of the regulars answered, "Thank you, five."

As the company dispersed for a break, Shawna caught Hutch's eye. He winked at her and mouthed, "Congratulations."

Shawna's heart fluttered with happiness but also nerves. This new development had brought her one step closer to her secret dream of stardom, but what if Penny or another performer got sick, and she actually had to go on?

Judith wasn't happy to lose Shawna as a helper, but Shawna could not have been more over the moon at the change. For the remainder of the morning's rehearsal, Shawna sat on a stool at the edge of the stage, script in hand, penciling every blocking movement and character motivation in the margins. When dance rehearsal commenced after lunch, Shawna practiced far upstage to keep out of Penny's way. Penny shot hostile glances at Shawna when she wasn't struggling with the choreography, but Hutch smiled and gave her a *thumbs-up* when the rehearsal ended.

She had survived her first day on the job, and what an eventful day it had been!

Shawna was heading to the bathroom to freshen up before her bike ride home when she noticed Penny chatting with Dougal, the TD, in a corner of the backstage area, lit only by a dim blue light. Intrigued, Shawna ducked behind the upstage curtain, parting the gap just enough to observe the duo from afar. Penny leaned against the wall with one knee up, smiling seductively at Dougal. He shot a quick up and down the connecting corridors before moving toward her. Shawna caught her breath, convinced the scruffy TD would kiss the aging ingenue, but instead, he handed her a shopping bag. The shiny white bag looked like something from an upscale store, not exactly where she'd expect Dougal to shop; she quickly checked herself for being classist.

Penny's smile lengthened as she thanked Dougal with a peck on the cheek. He returned the smile and held open the backstage door for her, watching her trot off with lively steps into the sun-drenched parking lot. When Dougal turned back, Shawna hurried away and bumped straight into Hutch.

"What's your hurry, little lady?" Hutch's pearly whites glistened in the cool backstage darkness.

"Oh, just getting ready to leave." Shawna tried to appear calm and collected despite what she'd just witnessed. She wondered if Hutch knew what was going on between his girlfriend and Dougal, whatever that was.

"A bunch of us are going to General Greene Inn for drinks if you want to join in," Hutch said. His hair was damp from showering, and he smelled of Irish Spring.

Shawna responded with an enthusiastic yes.

"Do you need a ride?" Hutch asked.

Shawna brightened until she remembered her bicycle. "No thanks. I'll meet you there."

"Okay."

Hutch waved and continued toward the same door Penny had passed through, the one always propped up with the paint can until someone could change the lock. She wondered why Penny and Hutch didn't ride together. She'd have to query Judith for some details about their relationship. As strange and "difficult" as Judith was, she certainly appeared to be an authority on all the dirt.

## CHAPTER 6

The General Greene Inn, located just a mile from the theater, was Tullytown's oldest historical landmark, marking the exact spot where George Washington and Nathanael Greene plotted the historical Delaware River crossing in 1776. A bit of a history buff himself, RJ had for many years portrayed General Washington in the annual Battle of Trenton Christmas Day reenactment until an unfortunate fall from a horse led to a severe knee injury. After two orthopedic surgeries, RJ made a remarkable recovery and no longer required a cane, although he often carried the Shillelagh he purchased on vacation in Ireland for dramatic effect.

While RJ was at the bar entertaining a cluster of actors with a story about his juvenile days at Long Wharf, Shawna felt trapped by RJ's wife and leading lady, Liz, whom she made the mistake of joining in the corner booth. While Liz yammered about her physical ailments, including everything from gynecological issues to migraines, Shawna sipped a Coke with lemon and nodded politely. Shawna was still a month away from her twenty-first birthday, so there was no shot of rum in her drink. Not that she cared for any. Despite four years of college, she decided that alcohol, like sex, didn't appeal to her. She's often wondered if that made her a prude, or perhaps it made her wiser than her classmates. She'd heard too many horror stories about the overindulgence of both vices and was happy to avoid them.

Liz reached across the table and patted Shawna's hand.

"I'm so happy RJ cast you as Penny's understudy," Liz said in an exaggerated stage whisper.

Before responding, Shawna glanced at the bar to see if Penny was within earshot. The last thing she wanted was to stir up jealousy. But Penny was smiling, standing close to Hutch, engrossed in RJ's pontifications.

Liz's grip tightened on Shawna's wrist. "Oh, don't worry. She's sucking up to RJ like she always does. You know they're having an affair, don't you?"

"No, I didn't know." Shawna took another sip of Coke. She despised it when people burdened her with personal information despite barely knowing them. She recalled her discomfort when her college roommate confessed to an abortion their first night together in the dorm. It was information Shawna felt too inexperienced to carry, and she was relieved when the girl dropped out halfway through the first semester.

"Well," Liz said, releasing Shawna's hand and slugging down the rest of her Manhattan before signaling Eddie, the waiter, for another round. "It's been going on for years. She's not the first either."

"Oh." Shawna's toes curled beneath the table. She didn't want to hear anymore, mostly because she respected RJ and didn't want the knowledge of his infidelity to color her opinion of him.

While Liz nervously twisted her wedding band on her

swollen finger, Shawna thought it wise to change the subject. "Playing Clytemnestra must be such a wonderful challenge. I'd love to interview you for my college's alumni newsletter if you wouldn't mind."

Liz eyed Eddie anxiously, tapping her fingers against the empty glass. "Of course, dear. It's not the New York Times, but I'll do it as a favor to you." Her face softened when Eddie set down the glass.

"There you are, madam," Eddie said with a flourish.

"Thank you, my dear," Liz said. "Will you also bring us some house fries? Shawna, you'll eat some, won't you?"

Shawna wasn't hungry, but she told Liz sure.

"As I was saying," Liz fished the cherry out of the cocktail glass and bit down on it, "Penny has the tits but not the talent."

Shawna covered her mouth with her hand to keep from laughing.

"It's true. RJ's always been a tit man." She cast a regretful glance downward at her large breasts resting on the table-top. "You don't mind my bawdy talk, do you? In today's world, you must be careful not to offend anyone." Liz rolled her eyes dramatically. "Why, back in my day--what the!"

The old wooden booth swayed and creaked when Dougal crashed into the seat next to Liz.

"Damn you, Dougal, you spilled my fucking drink," Liz said. She picked up a cocktail napkin and blotted the front of her floral-patterned blouse.

"Sorry about that," grunted Dougal. He gazed at Shawna across the booth with the same zoned-out look she'd seen in the eyes of notorious campus stoners and their boyfriends; except Dougal's eyes were not only bloodshot, they were also focused on her with a lustful intensity which made her involuntarily clamp her thighs together beneath the table.

"You the fresh meat?" Dougal asked gruffly.

Liz burst out laughing and slapped Dougal's arm playfully. "You can't make jokes like that these days," slurred Liz. "Not with today's kids. Everyone's so damn woke!"

Dougal's eyelids narrowed in a way that appeared to Shawna very lizard-like. "Is that right?"

Liz took another long slurp of her drink.

"Don't get your panties in a twist," Dougal said, addressing Shawna. "Just joking around."

"I wasn't, I..." stumbled Shawna, annoyingly aware of the blush fanning her cheeks.

"It wasn't that long ago when *you* were the fresh meat," Liz said with a sidelong glance at Dougal.

Dougal snaked his arm around Liz's shoulder and said, "I remember it well, Lizzie baby. I remember it well."

Liz colored and laughed. "I'm sure you do."

*So*, thought Shawna, confused. *Does this mean Liz had an affair with Dougal?* A wave of revulsion passed through her at the thought of them together. *But if Liz was unfaithful, too, why is she upset about RJ? Isn't that a double standard? Maybe it's just the way things are in the theater.*

Dougal raked a hand through his hair and shouted across the bar. "Yo, Eddie. Bring me a Bud, will ya?" Shawna noticed the half-moons of dirt beneath his workingman fingers.

"Just a minute," returned Eddie tersely.

"And those fries, too!" called Liz. "Sprinkle some Old Bay on 'em too. Will ya, Eddie?"

"Listen, Mama." Dougal removed his arm from around Liz's shoulder, revealing a wet underarm stain on his t-shirt. He fished a Marlboro from his shirt pocket, eyed the No Smoking sign, made a face, and stuck it behind one ear. "If RJ wants me to risk my ass painting those fucking twenty-foot columns, I need a Genie. There's no getting around it."

"Here you go." Eddie plopped down the fries and the beer.

Liz picked up the catsup bottle and made a red spiral on top of the fries. "Talk to RJ about it."

"Yeah, I did that, and he keeps putting me off, which is why I'm talking to you. We don't have to buy one, just rent it for chrissakes. But I can't be walking up and down ladders with my fucking leg the way it is."

"What's a Genie?" asked Shawna.

Douglas took a pull on his beer, wiped his mouth with the back of his hand, and laughed. "You are green, ain't you?"

"Don't pick on Shawna, Dougal," said Liz, French fry mulch in her open mouth. "I'll talk to RJ tonight and see what I can do."

"You're the best, Liz." Dougal pounded down his beer, planted a wet kiss on Liz's check, belched loudly, and climbed out of the booth. Shawna was astounded when Liz actually blushed, or perhaps it was from the alcohol and Old Bay fries.

Dougal made for the side exit. Through the window by the booth, Shawna watched Dougal greet a man in his sixties in the parking lot. Their appearances were a study in contrasts: one shabby with greasy hair and questionable hygiene, the other in a neat shirt and tie with a thick mop of gray hair that looked suspiciously like a toupee in the outdoor light.

Shawna couldn't resist asking Liz if she knew who the older gentleman was.

"Oh, you mean Ron?"

"Ron?"

"Sure, Ron Dee. He works at the theater. Manager Director, a fancy title for chief pencil pusher. He works behind the scenes with Harriet, so you'll rarely see him. Unless something goes wrong, and then you'll never see him." Liz laughed at her own joke.

*So, that's the elusive Ron,* thought Shawna.

Shawna watched the two men chatting. It was apparent they had an easy rapport between them. Ron's gold lighter flashed in the late afternoon sun rays when he lit Dougal's cigarette. She recalled Judith's mention of some shady business with Ron and Dougal, and the weird exchange backstage with Penny was suspicious. She was about to connect some very unsavory dots when she reminded herself of something her Dad had once advised her. Being interested in people and their problems is fine if you can be of service. Otherwise, it's none of your damn business.

Deciding not to stoop to the level of idle gossip, if only in her mind, Shawna sipped her Coke to the bottom of the glass, reflecting idealistically about how the theater brought people together, from the highly educated to the high school drop-out, all working toward a common goal.

"Dougal and his Genie," Liz mumbled. A maudlin mask had replaced her buoyancy. "You know, that boy lapped up what was left of my youth and beauty. I don't think RJ even noticed." She huffed. "Or cared. Look at him, ever the *artiste*."

Shawna twisted in her seat to see RJ settling himself behind the tavern's baby grand piano. He set his drink on top and began playing a soft jazz number with considerable skill. Shawna turned back to Liz and noticed how miserable she looked with the ice melting in her cocktail glass and most of the French fries consumed.

Feeling sorry for her, Shawna asked about the Genie Dougal had mentioned. She wanted to know everything about the theater, including the technical aspects.

Liz twirled her fingers in the air. "Oh, that mechanical platform thing you can lower up and down to paint the scenery and hang lights and shit."

"Sounds dangerous. Is that how Dougal hurt his leg?"

Liz rolled her eyes. "No. He crashed his motorcycle last summer, drunk and stoned, of course. Luckily, no one else was hurt."

Liz fished the last ice cube from her glass and sucked on it. "At least Dougal's a *real* man. We don't get too many of them in the theater, kiddo. In case you haven't noticed."

"What about Hutch?" The words flew from Shawna's mouth before she could catch them. She hoped Liz was too inebriated to clock it.

Liz's glassy gaze sharpened. "I think someone has a crush."

Shawna's cheeks flushed. "Oh, please don't--"

"Tell anyone?" Liz shrugged. "Don't worry, kiddo. Your secret is safe with me, but--" she leaned forward across the table as much as her large breasts would allow and whispered, "the jury's still out if Hutch plays on our team, if you know what I mean."

*What? Hutch gay?*

Shawn craned her neck to catch Hutch leaning against the bar cradling a glass of white wine. He had changed from his rehearsal clothes to dark designer jeans and a spanking white v-neck t-shirt with a gold Versace logo. "He does dress very nice," Shawna said wistfully.

"Exactly," Liz croaked and waved down Eddie for another Manhattan.

Shawna bit her tongue at Liz's offensive statement and wondered how she could squirm away from her company without seeming rude. Finally, she told Liz she had to get home before dark and offered to pay for the Coke. But Liz waved her away, telling her she'd take care of the drinks and the fries. Shawna hadn't eaten any of the fries but kept that observation to herself. She couldn't help but feel pity for Liz and her apparent unhappiness.

*I guess that's what a bad marriage will do to you, which is why I intend to stay single until I'm at least thirty-five.*

Shawna popped out the side door into the parking lot and breathed the sweet country air deep into her lungs. She pedaled away from the General Greene Inn, feeling grateful for her youth and freedom. She avoided the main highway and took a rural back road, which extended the distance but was a much safer ride as twilight grayed the woods and fields. Her Dad would appreciate her caution.

It wasn't hard to see that the theater people, especially the older ones like RJ and Liz, had acted decadently in their youths and now seemed to be paying the price with damaged relationships and bad habits. She wondered if some of that decadence would rub off her and if that was necessarily bad. It's not like she set out to be Miss Goodie Two-Shoes, as one of her college classmates had mockingly called her once. It was just that she didn't see the sense in doing drugs, drinking herself silly, or indulging in casual sex with spoiled Penn frat boys. When the time came for her to get involved with a boy--no, man--she wanted it to be special and lasting, something like her parents had before cancer robbed them of their happy-ever-after.

Shawna tried not to think about her mother who was taken from her when she was just a freshman in high school. It seemed long ago to her, although she understood that for her Dad, it was only yesterday. She wondered if her conservative mother would approve of her growing crush on Hutch. Would she give her good advice in the ways of love, or tell her to wait, as she had, for the right man to come along?

*She was my age when she married my Dad. Am I ready to take that plunge?*

Her other crushes had been on older men, like the assistant professor in her English Lit class. She wasn't the only girl who'd had a crush on him, and when she heard he had married one of her classmates, she was livid with jealousy. That the girl dropped out of school and had a baby within six months of the wedding made Shawna wonder if that's what it took to get a man.

She veered off the road to an old cow path and bumped along the rutted trail until she had to cross a shallow stream that snaked its way behind her development. She and the other kids from the neighborhood used to catch crayfish there in the summer. Then, when they reached their teen years, those same kids would hang out in the same spot to drink 40s, smoke cigarettes, and even, sometimes, weed. That's when Shawna stopped hanging out with them.

She remounted her bike upon reaching the smooth cul-de-sac pavement.

*Maybe I'm being too cautious. Or perhaps I'm reserving myself for a truly extraordinary adventure. It feels like all the signs point to this being the summer it finally happens.*

Riding quickly toward her house, like a horse returning to the barn, she acknowledged her excitement, and also her fear.

## CHAPTER 7

From the high stool at the kitchen island, Shawna watched her Dad methodically grate a block of Parmesan cheese over the homemade pasta. She tried to keep up with the pre-dinner chatter about how Parma had the most delicious food in all of Italy and what wine best complemented the flavors. But beneath the counter, Shawna's toes were tapping out the latest dance routine Rex had taught her, and her head was filled with her favorite musical numbers from the show that she'd grown to love in the first two weeks of rehearsal. She'd caught the theater bug and caught it bad. However, to appease Bill's complaints that he never saw her anymore, she decided to have dinner at home for once instead of going out with the rest of the cast.

When Bill finished adding a dash of fresh parsley to the dish, he tossed a white linen dishtowel over his shoulder and said, "I thought we'd eat in the sunroom for a change."

Shawna hopped off the stool. "Okay, I'll set the table."

"Don't bother. I already took care of it. Just grab us two wine glasses."

"Really?" Shawna asked, pleasantly surprised. It was the first time her Dad had suggested she join him for a real drink.

"You're almost twenty-one. I won't tell if you won't," Bill said with a wink. He swooped up the dishes. "I'll come back for the salad."

The sunroom was, in reality, a screened-in porch with one glass wall lined with empty shelves where her Mom's herbs had once sat in handmade pottery. Shawna had tried to cultivate her own garden in her Mom's honor, but when the plants died from lack of care, she felt depressed and thus ended her attempts at horticulture.

Shawna took a bite of the sumptuous food and hummed with pleasure. "Wow, Dad. It's too much!"

"With all that dancing you've been doing, I figured the extra calories wouldn't hurt." He leaned back in his chair and rubbed his belly self-consciously. "But what's my excuse?"

Shawna laughed and sipped her wine. "You look great, Dad."

"Thanks." Bill took a sip, too. "So, now that I have you captive by my cuisine par excellence, why don't you tell me what's going on?"

Shawna shrugged. "What do you mean?"

She knew what he meant, but since joining the theater and discovering a new world both in and outside of herself, she wasn't eager to share it, not even with her Dad.

"Well, are you enjoying yourself?"

"Absolutely." She tore off a piece of garlic bread.

"What do they do there exactly?" Bill's cheeks were already flush from the wine.

"What do you mean, Dad?" She didn't like his tone. Despite his attempt at showing interest, she knew he hated the idea of his academically gifted daughter getting pulled in by the artsy crowd. "We're rehearsing a show. We work very hard."

"Work!" Bill scoffed, pouring more wine.

She knew they were about to have *that* conversation again, where he told her she should be thinking about graduate programs in engineering.

"Did they find that missing lady yet?" Shawna archly changed the subject.

Bill winced. "No, and that journalist chick--sorry--lady has been on my case for weeks about it."

"Her name's Candace something, right?" Shawna took a sip of her Chianti. She appreciated the wine's bite and understood why it was a good pairing with the meal's bold tastes. It certainly wasn't the drink any of her college friends would be guzzling through a funnel at a frat party.

"Uh-huh."

"So, you remember her?"

"No. Should I?"

"Well, as you've said many times, it's a very small town."

"Yeah, well, I wasn't mayor then, was I?"

Shawna noted the defensiveness in his voice.

"Dad, are you all right? Your face is red."

That couldn't be from only two glasses of wine. She'd spotted an empty bottle in the recycle bin earlier. Had he been drinking all evening?

He lazily waved a hand in the air and smiled. "I'm just irritated that the DA wants to open the case. It's a waste of time."

"But what about the car they found? Were they any clues?"

"Clues of what?" He laughed and reached for more bread. "That she was murdered?"

"Well, it's possible, isn't it?"

"Possible, but highly unlikely. That lady probably dumped her own car and took off with a boyfriend or something."

"Seems like an odd thing to do."

"Not odd if you knew she lived with elderly parents who were a burden for her to care for. Maybe she wanted to send them to an early grave by worrying them to death."

"Ah-ha! So, you did know her."

"No. I just know about the case. Don't you have rehearsal tonight?"

"Just dance rehearsal. I'm not required to be there, but I can go and watch."

Bill sank back in the chair and emptied the rest of the wine into his glass. "Why don't you go watch it then? I have some work to do tonight anyway." He sounded tired. Was it the result of the wine, the heavy meal, or the conversation?

"Don't you want me to clean up?"

"Nah. You run along."

Shawna stood and placed her napkin next to her plate. "Well, thanks for dinner, Dad. It was great."

As she walked away, he slurred. "If you're taking my car, use the back roads. You've been drinking."

*You're a fine one to give advice*, she thought.

"I'll ride my bike," she called back.

He didn't answer, but when she turned, she saw him slumped at the table. Her heart pinged at how old he looked beneath the rattan chandelier. She guessed he'd been holding onto a lot of sadness since losing her mom, sadness he mostly kept to himself.

As she pedaled out of the neighborhood, Shawna thought, with a tinge of guilt, about how, now that she was older, all the adults in her life, the people she once looked up to as godly figures, were revealing themselves to be flawed, even tragic characters.

*Maybe that's why I love the theater*, she thought as she cautiously crossed the highway. Characters may be flawed, but at the end of the play, there is always a resolution, whether happy or tragic. Eager to leave behind the heaviness of the evening, she welcomed a cool breeze, which seemed to lift her from behind and gently push her toward a new destiny.

## CHAPTER 8

"Five, six, seven, eight!" Rex cried out the counts so many times that evening, he sounded hoarse. Shawna was content to just watch the great choreographer at work, but Rex insisted that she practice onstage and shadow Penny's moves. "Your muscles need to learn it more than your brain," he told her.

Shawna was pleased with herself for catching on quickly. Penny, however, continued to struggle with the choreography. She kept turning in the wrong direction, and when she collided with Hutch on a crossover, she lost it.

"I can't focus with that bitch moving behind me upstage!" Penny cried before sinking to the floor and holding her ankle as if her old injury had flared up.

*Bitch?* Shawna stopped dancing and stared angrily at the back of Penny's peroxided head. *Does she mean me?*

Rex clapped his hands together. The sound echoed through the empty house. "All right. Everyone, take five."

"Five minutes!" Blake announced.

"Thank you, five," a few tired voices echoed back.

Rex waved a finger at Penny and said, "Let's talk." From

the tightness of Rex's mouth, Shawna guessed he wasn't happy with Penny's outburst, and yet when he spoke to her privately, he seemed to be supportive, patiently stroking her arm while Penny fought back tears.

Shawna slipped through the gap in the upstage curtain to hide her own tears, now brimming to the surface. She tried so hard to be respectful and stay out of Penny's way, yet Penny continued to harass her. Her internship would be perfect if it weren't for her. It just wasn't fair. Grabbing fistfuls of the curtains, she buried her face in the soft darkness, wishing she could disappear, if only for a moment.

She sensed a presence behind her. Embarrassed and flustered, she turned to see Hutch, so close she could feel his warmth.

"Hey," he whispered. "Don't mind Penny. She's just insecure. You threaten her, that's all."

"Me? Threatening?" Shawna's voice squeaked. "But I'm a nobody."

He leaned in so close she could smell his Tic Tac breath and a whiff of spicy cologne. "You are far from a nobody. You're very talented and pretty." His deep voice was balm to her tattered nerves, not to mention ego.

Encouraged by his words, Shawna gazed up at Hutch with moist eyes. The glow of the blue backstage lights bathed half his face in deep shadow. Shawna was reminded of Hutch's performance as the Phantom a few seasons back. She thought he was fantastic in the role.

She wondered if everyone, including herself, played a role in their daily lives. Her Dad, for instance, played the role of town mayor, but who was he really?

*Maybe we need theater because we need the illusion of art to uncover the truth behind the mask.*

She was on the verge of expressing her philosophical

thoughts to Hutch when she noticed him moving closer. As his manly presence drew her toward him like a magnet, a tingling sensation started in her loins and spread to her fingertips and hair follicles. She was transported to the Paris Opera House, and she was Christine, about to be lured into the Phantom's dark seduction. For a moment, she was sure he was going to kiss her.

Rex's loud clap broke the spell. Shawna and Hutch jumped apart just as Penny crashed through the gap in the curtain and into Hutch's arms.

"Everyone's being so mean to me," Penny complained, a sob hitching in her throat.

"You'll get the moves down, baby," Hutch said. "You're putting too much pressure on yourself."

While Penny buried her face in Hutch's chest, he glanced at Shawna over the blonde's head and slowly touched his lips with his finger as if to say *let's keep this little moment between us*.

Still dazed from the encounter, Shawna backed away quietly, feeling her way along the curtain en route to the bathroom to splash some water on her face.

"You look like you've seen a ghost," Judith said when they passed in the hall.

"I'm not sure I haven't," Shawna said, thinking about the imaginary Phantom's strange hold over her.

Shawna instantly regretted her reply to Judith because she became aware that Judith, who needed little encouragement to start a conversation, was trailing her to the bathroom.

Judith settled in the bathroom, leaning against the wall beside the sink while Shawna used the stall.

"The ghost of Candace Laherty haunts this place. I know, because I've seen her."

"Really, Judith?"

"Did you know that Candace Laherty and I were in the same graduating class?" Judith talked through the stall while Shawna used the toilet. Acutely embarrassed by the sound of her urine stream, Shawna flushed twice, missing some of Judith's monologue. "We weren't close friends, but we stayed in touch after high school. She wanted nothing more than to be an actress. But if she had asked me, which she didn't, I'd have told her she was wasting her time. She couldn't even get cast in our high school productions. No talent. But try convincing someone who's made up her mind. I don't think she left town at all. If you want my opinion, she was murdered."

That caught Shawna's attention. Perhaps Judith had some information she could pass on to her Dad. "But why would someone kill her?"

Shawna left the stall and squeezed some pink hand soap from the dispenser. She noticed the paper towel dispenser was empty.

"Ha!" Judith laughed. "Ask her married boyfriend that question."

"Who was that?"

Judith shrugged. "Hell if I know. It was all a big secret at the time. But someone knows the real story."

Shawna shook her head. "Sorry, I don't believe in ghosts."

Judith screwed up her face in what Shawna thought was a very unattractive scowl. "Says the new kid on the block."

"Judith, I don't mean to offend you and I understand there are superstitions around any old building, especially theaters, but the idea that there's a ghost here is simply preposterous.

Judith's hands rested defiantly on her hips. "Shows how much you know."

Shawna opened a corner closet to look for more paper towels. She realized it was senseless to speak reason to someone like Judith. Of course, ghosts weren't real. "Maybe Candace Laherty left town for some other reason."

"Yeah, and maybe you're stupid!"

Shawna spun around in time to see Judith hurrying out the door.

"Jesus," Shawna muttered. "Some people..."

In the closet, she found a roll of paper towels next to a dusty Tampax box and some ancient pink hair gel called Dippity-do. She wondered when the last time the theater had been cleaned and if anyone had spoken to Ron about it.

∽

SHAWNA MOVED AS FAR upstage as possible for the remainder of the rehearsal. After much patience from Rex and support from the other actors, Penny finally learned the routine, if not flawlessly, at least adequately.

The heavy pasta dinner, the wine, the bike ride, and the hours of dancing had left Shawna exhausted, so she was thrilled to see her Dad seated in the front row at the end of rehearsal, smiling at her and looking like himself again.

"Come on, honey," he said. "I don't want you riding home in the dark. We'll throw your bike in the trunk."

After the encounters with Penny and Hutch, the chatting about ghosts, and Judith's rudeness around the topic, Shawna was happy to throw off the weight of a long day and let her Dad take care of things. She couldn't wait to crawl into bed.

**CHAPTER 9**

Shawna pedaled into the theater parking lot the next day, refreshed from a good night's sleep and an invigorating bike ride. From the way the blazing sunlight fired up the morning dew, she could tell the day would be hot. Whatever the weather, the world seemed perfect to Shawna. However, as she entered the theater space, she felt a sense of tragedy enveloping her like a dark cloak. She looked around, noting how the usual lively vibe had altered. And where did everyone go?

She was about to check her phone to see if she had missed a change in the schedule when a hand shot out and grabbed her arm.

Shawna screeched.

"Relax. It's just me."

"Judith," Shawna sighed with relief. "You scared--"

"Sh." Judith pressed a finger to Shawna's lips. Her finger smelled like onions. "Didn't you hear?"

"Uh, no. I just got here. Is everything all right?"

Grimly shaking her head, Judith pulled Shawna through the side exit door into the already blinding sunlight.

"What's going on?" Shawna asked, annoyed to be outside in the burgeoning heat.

"RJ got fired by the board last night."

"What?" Shawna couldn't believe it.

*Rick Jennings is Tullytown Players.*

"They can't do that!"

Judith huffed. "Well, they certainly can and did!"

"But why?"

Judith's lips curled with delight as she told the story of how RJ got drunk at the General Greene Inn the previous night, how he had fallen down the stairs on his way back from the men's room and had crashed into Eddie, the waiter, causing him to spill a tray of drinks all over a crowded table.

"That's awful," Shawna said.

"And it gets worse. He drove home!"

"Uh oh."

"Uh oh is right. Crashed his car into the 'Welcome Friend' sign on Main Street."

"Oh, shit!" Spontaneous laughter burst from Shawna's lips before she could draw it back. Her Dad had worked his ass off commissioning that stupid sign.

"You might think it's a barrel of laughs, but I happen to care about this town and this theater." Judith's face looked drawn in the bright sunlight, her faint mustache glistened with sweat.

"I'm sorry, Judith. Is RJ okay?"

"Oh, except for a hangover, he's fine. But the board has had enough, and I don't blame them."

"Poor Liz," said Shawna. "How's she doing?"

"Oh, running around like the May Queen, pretending nothing's wrong. She's the one who has the prob--"

The door popped open. Blake stuck her head out and barked at Shawna. "You're wanted on stage, now!"

Shawna jumped. "If RJ's gone, who's directing the show?"

Blake squinted as she held open the door. "That would be Dudley Wicks, and he doesn't tolerate lateness."

"Shit," muttered Shawna, rattled by the changing of the guard and what that might mean for her place in the company. Her eyes adjusted to the darkness as she hurried to the stage where the entire cast had assembled, quiet as church mice.

"So happy you could join us," Wicks said pointedly from center stage. His gaze bore into Shawna as she quickly filed in beside the others. "I realize this theater and this company are far from professional," his voice dripped arrogance, "but my background is the professional theater, so I will treat all of you like professionals, meaning I expect you to do your jobs and do them well."

Shawna looked around and noticed Liz wasn't there. With a shudder, she wondered if she had been fired, too.

"Now," Wicks continued. "If you focus very hard and work your little butts off, we'll all get through this process in one piece. Hopefully, I can salvage my play before opening night."

Shawna needed clarification. She thought RJ and Wicks were close friends. Despite the friendly camaraderie, sometimes she got the impression that anyone in the theater was a potential Iago, not to be trusted.

Wicks began the day's rehearsal by running through the scenes in which Liz didn't appear. But because Clytemnestra was a significant character, they ran out of material well before noon. Blake announced the lunch break an hour earlier than usual. The stress of losing RJ had killed Shawna's appetite, so she volunteered to help Judith dig out some period costumes from the storage unit in the hayloft. She didn't care for Judith's erratic outbursts, but her Dad had instructed her on the importance of getting along with all team members.

"The janitor and the secretary are as important as the CEO, and they usually know more than him," Mayor Bill had advised her on many occasions.

The enormous barn that housed the theater was a complicated maze, and Judith's directions on how to find the storage made it even more confusing for Shawna.

"Here's what you do," Judith instructed. "Go to the end of the stage left hallway, where you'll see an exit sign. Ignore it and turn right, go past the old cow cages until you see the cow head..."

"Cow head?" Shawna shivered.

"Yeah. The one from Gypsy." Judith cackled. "What do you think it was a real cow head?"

"But the cow cages are real?"

"Of course they're real. This used to be a barn. Remember?"

"Sure. Okay. Please continue."

"Well, like I was saying before I was rudely interrupted," huffed Judith. "Ignore the cow and go about ten paces till you reach a ladder on your left. You're going to climb three stories to the attic."

"You want me to climb three stories?"

"You're in shape, aren't you?"

"I guess."

"So, what's the problem? You're not afraid of the ghost, are you?"

Shawna laughed. "Don't be silly. There's no problem at all."

"Great. So, you're going to climb all the way to the top.

Pray the light bulb still works, but if not, there's a door you can slide open. It may be a bit rusty and there's a two-story drop on the other side, so just be careful you don't fall out." Judith mimed a falling body followed by a loud SPLAT.

"Fine. I got it," Shawna said, although none of it sounded very fun. But then, she thought about RJ's first-day speech, about how each of them is a link in a chain, and the weakest link could break the chain. She was determined not to be that weak link but a trooper always.

Bidding goodbye to Judith and trying to remember her convoluted directions, Shawna wandered into the barn's dark, backstage environs. When she turned to use the far upstage hallway, she ran into Dougal, who stood before an open fuse box wearing a headband with an LED light attached to it.

"Hey, baby," he said with a lecherous grin.

"I'm not a baby," Shawna replied.

He blocked her egress with an outstretched arm composed of ropey muscles and ugly tattoos. "Oh, don't tell me you're one of those."

"One of what?"

"Those stuck-up college types who think their shit don't stink."

*What a pig.*

"Excuse me," she said, shouldering past him.

"Hey," Dougal called after her. "You copped a feel just now. I can report you for sexual harassment." His sarcastic laughter chased her down the dimly-lit hallway that smelled increasingly of straw and manure.

As lowly as the task at hand was, Shawna welcomed some time away from the likes of Dougal. She considered reporting *him* for sexual harassment. She remembered reading the theater's strict policy about discrimination when she signed her employment paperwork.

*Was it all just for show?*

She recalled Dougal and Liz's tight connection, very tight if her assumptions were correct. She decided it was best not to stir the pot by reporting the exchange. Besides, the morning's rehearsals had been draining and she couldn't handle anymore drama. Wicks worked them like a drill sergeant and he never issued any compliments or words of encouragement the way RJ did. Already, it felt like a completely different production.

Occupied by her thoughts, Shawna didn't realize she was lost in the barn's inner maze until her forehead parted a string of cobwebs bowing down from the ceiling. Her feet made circles on the dusty floorboards as she tried to recall Judith's exact words. A cold hand touched her wrist, making her jump.

"Oh, I didn't mean to frighten you," said the calm voice.

Shawna recovered her composure and saw Harriet smiling up at her from her wheelchair.

"Sorry. I-I just didn't expect to see anyone down here."

"Well," said Harriet, her eyes twinkling and friendly behind her rhinestone-studded eyeglasses. "This part of the building can be pretty confusing. If you are trying to get back to the stage--"

"Actually, I was looking for the hayloft ladder."

Harriet appeared confused, prompting Shawna to explain the mission Judith had sent her on.

"Good ole Judith." Harriet chuckled. "Always making things more complicated than they need to be." Harriet rotated her wheelchair and pointed in the direction she had just come from. "You're almost there. See the cow head on top of the steamer trunk? The ladder is just past it."

"Ah, yes," Shawna said, slightly embarrassed. "Thanks, Harriet."

"You're welcome, dear."

Shawna followed Harriet's wheelchair tracks along the dusty floor, wondering what Harriet was doing in the nether regions of the barn.

"You're almost there," Harried called after her.

Shawna turned to wave and noted Harriet staring at her, a wide grin on her face. Perhaps the poor lady didn't realize how ghostly white she looked bathed in the shaft of sunlight sifting in through a gap in the wall. Shawna continued on, noting more gaps in the walls. Seeing how a large section of the barn remained unfinished, she understood now why they closed the theater during the winter season. It would require a major renovation to heat the building, not to mention the cost.

At last, Shawna reached the *Gypsy* cow head. At least someone had made the effort to protect it from the elements. Its cartoon face smiled at her through clear plastic wrapping, layered with dust.

Thinking that it must have been a while since the theater mounted a production of *Gypsy*, Shawna discovered the old wooden ladder. Mounted to the wall with thick rusty nails, the rungs were worn in the center by the tread of many farmers. The scent of the barn's original purpose was thick here, and if she closed her eyes, she could almost hear the livestock in their stalls rattling their harnesses.

*Might as well get on it with it.*

She climbed, pausing at the second story to catch her breath. The air she sucked in was thick and musty. Light pouring through one small window with a cracked pane revealed rusted toolboxes and a Victorian buggy.

By the time she reached the top floor, she was sweating

through her t-shirt. She flipped the light switch, and a single dusty bulb blazed from the apex of a sharply slanted roof dripping with cobwebs. Shawna looked around and sighed in the hot, dusty air that smelled of old straw and mold.

Costumes, rotting like fruit on the vine, stretched to infinity on rusty metal racks.

*Am I really supposed to find anything up here?*

Once her eyes adjusted to the dim light, she saw, to her relief, that the garments were arranged in some semblance of order. Perhaps, in the early days, a more energetic Judith had arranged everything according to plays and periods.

*Oklahoma* gingham dresses gave way to moth-eaten Civil War uniforms, faded *Brigadoon* tartans, and, at last, a rack of classical robes.

Shawna began pulling the freshest-looking costumes from the rack, thinking how using such old garments made about as much sense as creating a musical from a Greek tragedy.

*But what do I know?*

The hayloft was stifling, and after carrying two large piles of costumes to the top of the ladder, Shawna was gasping for breath. She worried that rehearsal had started again. Wicks wouldn't be pleased if she were late. She might even be fired from the understudy role. After all, look what happened to RJ. Deciding that there was a fine line between trooper and chump, Shawna vowed to be less officious.

"One more armful, and then I'm out of here."

Shawna had only walked a few steps toward the racks again when the light bulb exploded with a flash and a crack, leaving her stranded in complete darkness.

## CHAPTER 10

Shawna loosened her grip on the bundle of costumes, letting them tumble to the floor. Losing her orientation in the darkness, she was scared to walk in any direction lest she fall through the ladder opening. Gazing up, she saw dust motes swirling in the faint beams of light piercing the roof, but everywhere else was impenetrable darkness. She struggled to calm her racing heart and throbbing head as she calculated her next move.

She was listening to her own breath when a scream pierced the silence, causing panic to rise from her heart to her throat and wedge itself there. She sniffed the air and detected a burning smell. Maybe it was just the shattered light bulb, but a burning smell in an old barn was a harbinger of disaster. She remembered her recent conversation with her Dad about the theater being a dangerous firetrap. The timbers were dry, he'd said, and the electrical system was terribly outdated. She needed to get out of there now!

Did that scream mean someone was hurt? Burnt maybe? More reason for getting out of the barn now! Moving as if in slow motion, Shawna searched for the ladder opening. One wrong move, and she'd plummet three stories to her death.

Then she spotted a glimmer of hope--sunlight outlining the hayloft door Judith had mentioned. Shawna cautiously felt her way to the wall and searched desperately for a latch.

Another scream, much closer now, shocked her nerves. Shawna banged helplessly on the door, shouting, "Can anybody hear me?"

After some futile banging and a painful splinter wedging itself into the palm of her hand, she realized it was a sliding door, like the ones she'd seen on many old Tullytown barns. With a groan, she gripped the door's edge and shoved it sideways as hard as possible. Sunlight flooded in, almost blinding her with its brightness. Blinking into the blazing daylight, she saw the parking lot below, the big willow tree, and beyond that, the rolling fields of the farmland.

Invigorated by the fresh air, she shouted, "Hello! I'm trapped up here!"

There was the sound of the backdoor banging open and more screaming. Gazing down, she watched Penny bolt across the parking lot with Hutch giving chase.

*What's happening?*

When Penny reached the grass, she collapsed; Hutch sank to his knees beside her.

"Hey, Hutch! Penny! I'm up here!"

The theater's fire alarm sounded, drowning out her voice with its shrill blare.

*The barn is on fire! Maybe Penny's hurt.*

Since leaping from the third story into the abyss wasn't an option, Shawna swiftly made her way past the pile of costumes to the ladder opening, visible now in the fan of sunlight. It took all the patience she could muster to descend the ladder carefully to avoid slipping and falling.

However, once her feet hit the ground, she bolted toward the nearest exit, the sound of the fire alarm galvanizing her steps.

An acrid, burning stench stopped her in her tracks. Smoke billowed from the left upstage wing.

*Am I running straight into the fire?*

She was about to backtrack and search for another exit when she saw the source of the smell. At first, she thought it was a pile of costumes that had somehow ignited, but as she gazed closely through the smoke, she saw what it was and reeled back in horror.

Dougal lay twisted on the floor beneath the open fuse box he'd been working on. Noxious smoke poured out of the fuse box, forming a black cloud in the air. Dougal's face and hands were horribly charred. His eyes looked like hollow holes spewing yellow ooze. His mouth gaped open, revealing a protruding black tongue.

Shawna folded forward in shock and terror. The smoke burned her eyes; her throat closed against breathing in the toxic fumes. She had just begun to cough and retch when someone grabbed her from behind. Only after she was outdoors and breathing fresh air did she realize it was RJ who had rushed her to safety.

*But wasn't RJ fired? My God! What happened to Dougal?*

Her thoughts were a mangled delirium in a whirl of chaos and fear. Later, when she had time to process what had happened, she realized that she had dissociated from the shock until she'd found herself on the shaded grass beneath the willow tree. Glancing up, dazed, she saw RJ pacing the parking lot and shouting into his phone.

"I repeatedly told that goddam board about that electrical wiring," RJ bellowed, "But they wouldn't listen!"

Shawna looked around at the traumatized company

members strewn about the grass and parking lot, all in various stages of shock. Shawna was relieved to see that Harriet had made it out. She appeared to be in shock, a handkerchief pressed to her mouth. Ron was there too, looking ashen as he smoked a cigarette a few paces away. Blake leaned against the hood of her pickup, rubbing her eyes from smoke, tears, or both.

Shawna stood slowly, wondering if there was anything she could do to help. Penny was still on the ground, being comforted by Hutch. Shawna caught his eye, but he only shook his head sadly and looked away. She glanced at the building. Gray smoke sifted through the back door, but so far there were no flames. Her ears detected the faint wail of sirens in the distance.

Two Tullytown fire trucks, sirens blaring and lights flashing, sped down the gravel lane trailing dust clouds. An ambulance and two patrol cars followed close behind.

Acting as if he was still in charge, RJ loudly barked out orders at everyone to make room for the first responders. The electrical outage could have caused a fire somewhere else in the building, and they needed to check it out.

As Tullytown's finest rushed inside, Liz, who had just pulled up in her car, flung herself weeping into RJ's arms, practically knocking him to the ground.

Blake had recovered enough to do a company head count. Shawna heard her tell RJ that all personnel and cast were accounted for--everyone except for Dougal, and Dudley Wicks.

Curious, Shawna quickly scanned the mayhem and located Rex, whom she knew was Wick's friend. Showing tension in his muscular body, Rex stood apart from the others and was engaged in a private phone conversation. Shawna wondered if he was speaking with Wicks, or perhaps his agent, demanding to be released from his contract with this backwoods operation with its faulty wiring and deathtrap haylofts. Surely, Actor's Equity would shut down the theater once word of what had happened spread, and her Dad would get his wish to turn the property into a housing development. Tears flooded her eyes at the thought of so much lost in a single, horrible tragedy. And to think she had just spoken to Dougal. Could she have handled the situation with more kindness and understanding?

Much of this concern left her when she spotted her Dad's vehicle barreling down the driveway toward the theater. He must have heard the news on his scanner. As soon as her Dad climbed out of the car, Shawna leaped into his arms and cried like a baby.

∾

Mayor Bill decided to stick around while the Coroner and the Fire Marshall completed their work at the scene. It wasn't every day that Tullytown had a tragedy on this scale, or a missing person for that matter. Yet somehow, both mysterious events involved the theater. Shawna wondered grimly if the theater was cursed or, as Judith had suggested, haunted.

After declaring Shawna too upset to ride her bike home, Bill gave her the keys to the Lexus and told her not to worry about dinner. He'd catch a ride with one of the police officers and grab some take-out on his way home. For the first time, Shawna couldn't wait to drive away from the theater. Her former sanctuary had become a house of horrors. She doubted she could ever shake off that picture of Dougal's face in her mind. Clutching the keys, she hurried to the

Lexus, relieved to be out of there before they dragged Dougal out in a body bag. Blake and RJ were standing close to the car when she overheard a bit of their conversation.

"Where the hell's Wicks?" RJ asked.

Blake answered, "I haven't the faintest idea, but he's the one who insisted Dougal work on the electricity without powering down."

"For fuck's sake, why?"

"He didn't want to miss rehearsal time. I told him not to do it--" Blake, uncharacteristically overcome with emotions, covered her face with her hands and wept. Shawna guessed that she and Dougal were friends, that some of these relationships at the theater went back years, decades.

RJ gripped Blake's shoulders as if to shake her out of her distress. "Whatever you do, don't tell the Fire Marshall about it, or they'll close us down for good. Don't worry about Wicks. I'll deal with him."

RJ and Blake clammed up when they saw Shawna walking up to her Dad's vehicle.

Shawna wondered if the look of sympathy RJ shot her was sincere. "Be well, Shawna," RJ said. "And don't worry about anything."

Blake mumbled something to herself as she fetched a cigarette from the pocket of her jeans.

Shawna drove away, moist palms on the steering wheel, wondering if she should tell her Dad what she had overheard. If Wicks had caused such a safety breach, the town council might use it as an excuse to close the theater. She sensed her Dad would jump at any chance to make that happen, and acting to defend public safety would be a convenient justification.

Shawna decided to keep the information to herself, for now. She spent what was left of an awful day soaking in her family's backyard pool, happy to wash away the sweat and dust and to cleanse her nostrils of the horrible, lingering stench.

After she had taken a shower and changed into her comfiest PJs, she padded out to the kitchen to get a cold drink. Her Dad texted her to say he'd be home late. The town council was going to have an emergency board meeting over the theater's fate.

With so much hanging in the balance, Shawna could barely swallow the leftovers she'd heated up. After hours of scrolling through streaming platforms and settling on nothing that would distract her, she fell asleep on the sofa beneath the quilt her mother had crocheted. An exhausted Bill woke her after midnight to tell her that the theater would be closed for two weeks while new wiring was installed. Dudley Wicks was fired without incident, and RJ was again at the helm.

Dragging the quilt behind her like a child, Shawna left the family room to head upstairs, leaving Bill sitting in his comfy chair, nursing a beer and grumbling about the additional costs for the theater's renovations.

In bed that night, Shawna privately rejoiced at the turn of events. Despite what happened to Dougal, she was glad Wicks was out and RJ was back. Now, with the theater shutting down for two weeks, she had more time to learn all the female roles. As the day's events had hideously illustrated, anything can happen in the theater.

That night, Shawna had her first actor's nightmare, one where she stood in the wings nervously waiting for her entrance to play a role she didn't know. She looked down, expecting to see herself clad in a costume, when she saw with a flash of panic and intense shame, that she was completely naked. Someone shoved her from behind, and she stumbled onto the stage into a pool of bright lights. An actor stood next to her down center. He wore Agamemnon's costume, but when he turned toward her, she saw that it was Dougal's charred faced wearing a hideous grin. His eyes were empty sockets dripping yellow pus.

A few days later, she stood with the rest of the company at Dougal's unconventional funeral service. Despite the scorching weather, Liz was dressed in full mourning attire. She openly sobbed as Dougal's biker friends scattered his ashes into the Delaware River. However, a gust of wind blew most of the ashes back onto the riverbank, with some landing on Liz's intricate black lace veil. Shawna looked away, deciding it was best not to alert her.

## CHAPTER 11

In the days following the tragedy, the theater's fate was the talk of the town. Mayor Bill spent long hours at the office and after-hours meetings. Most nights, he came home too exhausted to do much except flop on the family room sectional and scroll through sports programs.

Shawna took over cooking duties, and although she was not as talented as her Dad in that department, she enjoyed learning about different foods and seasonings. Eager to expand her knowledge beyond the internet, she pulled a few of her Mom's old cookbooks off the shelf and discovered a wooden box containing hand-written recipes on index cards. Shawna stroked the elegant scroll in fading ink with a rising lump in her throat. Her Mom had started life with such hope, only to have a disease cruelly snatch it from her.

To honor her Mom's memory, Shawna prepared chicken cacciatore, which her Mom had earmarked as one of her Dad's favorites. When her Dad lumbered in at eight p.m., exhausted from another meeting, she relished the look of delight on his face when he breathed in the good cooking smells wafting from the kitchen.

"This is delicious," he said, going for a second helping. "Maybe I should have sent you to cooking school instead of college.

Shawna chuckled. "Maybe you should have. I used Mom's old recipe, you know."

"I knew there was something." Bill lowered his fork to his plate and gazed at the Anthony's Blue Italian wedding china.

"I'm sorry, Dad. I-I didn't mean to upset you."

He reached across the table and patted her hand. "You didn't, hon. It's just been a long day."

They resumed their meal, chitchatting about Italian cooking, arguing the merits of both Northern and Southern Italian cooking, but Bill's eyes remained distant throughout the meal.

Deciding she probably should do more with her time than cook, Shawna made good on her promise to interview Liz for her college's alumni magazine. She chose a sunny but cool morning to ride her bike through the cul-de-sac where her house sat and then traverse a shaded path through the woods to Tullytown proper.

The few cafés, real estate offices, and nail salons that dotted Main Street always made Shawna yearn for more activity--a bookstore or music shop would be nice. Still, the street held a quaint allure, and several of the shopkeepers had added cheer to their storefronts with potted plants and flowerbeds.

Main Street t-boned Tullytown's Riverview Drive, where stately Victorian homes, many lovingly restored and painted in muted jewel tones, sat majestically on the riverbank's high bluff. Shawna often fantasized about residing in one of those beauties, especially the forest green mansion with the widow's walk and twin cupolas, which was the emerald jewel in the crown. Unfortunately, her Dad preferred modern conveniences and new construction. But these old "white elephants," as he called them, harkened back to a time when Tullytown was the stomping ground of industrial tyrants and their fashionable wives. Looking at those old homes filled Shawna with romance, like how she felt when she first stepped inside the theater.

The Jennings' house wasn't the grandest of the group, but its pale purple paint and stained-glass windows certainly made an impression. Shawna felt a tingle of apprehension when she pedaled up the Jennings' driveway. The lawn was overgrown; the rose bushes needed tending. She wondered if the yard's neglect indicated that RJ and Liz were still reeling from the tragedy and that she should postpone the visit. But all her misgivings were brushed aside when Liz opened the door with a bright coral lipstick smile and folded Shawna in a big hug as if it had been years since they'd last met.

After the effusive greeting, Shawna trailed Liz, clad in a floating floral caftan, through a narrow center hall. The house was cramped and not very clean. Books and magazines were stacked everywhere, even on the carpeted stairs. An Angora cat, that Liz introduced as Juliet, emerged from behind a large Chinese urn containing a sickly-looking spider plant. The dusty furniture appeared antique to Shawna's untrained eyes, and somewhere in the house was a litter box that needed emptying. Shawna was relieved when Liz led her to a screened-in back porch where the air was fresher. It faced a small, overgrown garden and the Delaware River beyond.

Liz plopped down on a well-worn floral loveseat with Juliet in her lap while Shawna settled into a wobbly wicker chair.

Shawna pulled her iPhone from the pocket of her jean shorts and said, "Is it okay if I record our conversation?"

"Of course. Go right ahead," Liz said. "Oh, I forgot to offer you water. RJ!" Liz's screech was so loud Shawna flinched and nearly dropped her phone. "I forgot he's at that damn town hall meeting." Liz started to hoist herself from the loveseat.

"Oh, I don't need any water."

"Are you sure?"

"Positive."

Liz settled back. "This thing with the theater is such a nightmare. And I hate to say this, Shawna, but your father's blocking every advancement."

Shawna winced. "I know, and I'm sorry. I think he's just worried about the budget."

Liz smiled indulgently. "I get it. Money is money, but there is no Tullytown without Tullytown Players! The restaurants and motels depend on the business it brings to the community, for starters."

Shawna knew of only a few restaurants in town, and the only hotel was a seedy Knights Inn on the main highway. Still, she decided it was best not to argue.

Before Shawna could recite any of her prepared questions, Liz launched into a monologue about her days as a young actress in New York. She spoke, at length, about how she understudied the role of Stella in a Broadway production of *Streetcar*. When the star got sick, she went on for a Wednesday matinee and performed the role flawlessly.

"So, you see, Shawna," Liz said with a pointing finger. "You never know when your big break will come."

Liz went on about how she'd impressed the director so much she was offered the touring company role when the original actress bowed out. Also in the company, playing the role of Mitch, was a young actor named Richard Jennings. They didn't date immediately, as RJ was married to someone else then.

This was news to Shawna.

"We were both eventually cast in an Off-Broadway production of *Private Lives*," Liz said as she fluffed a sofa cushion. "And that's when we fell in love. And together, we came up with the mad idea of opening a summer stock theater in Reynold's old barn. Tullytown property was cheap in those days. Next thing we knew, we bought this house, and the rest, as they say, is history."

"And you have no regrets about leaving Broadway?" Shawna reminded herself that a good journalist isn't afraid to ask tough questions.

"What you need to understand, Shawna," Liz said, stroking Juliet. "Is that when RJ and I started our careers, Broadway producers mounted interesting new plays every season. Then, all of a sudden, it's musical after musical, and then those stupid movies turned into musicals starring some stupid TV star." She shuddered with contempt. "And don't even get me started on the audience. *The Great White Way* has become the great white bread way. Those suburbanites with fanny packs couldn't sit through a play by Miller or O'Neil if their lives depended on it. All they want is mindless entertainment--Disneyland in New York! And if you ask me, it's for the birds!"

"Well, what makes Tullytown Players different?" Shawna asked to ease Liz into a more positive spin for the article.

Liz brightened. "Our theater is what the Shubert in New Haven used to be before they sold out. We're the only theater on the East Coast that takes chances with new, at times experimental, material."

"Like Dudley Wicks' *Agamemnon*?"

"Nice segue, kid," Liz said with a wink. "You know, I think you have a good shot at a theater career?"

"Really?"

"Sure. You're young and talented, smart and pretty." She sighed and ran a finger under her sagging chin. "We all start that way."

The side door clanged open. Juliet bounded off Liz's lap and padded out of the room to investigate.

"RJ?" Liz called.

A tired voice boomed back. "Yes, it's me. This goddamn town and its stupid bureaucracy."

"Be on your best behavior. Shawna's back here."

"Who?"

"Shawna, the Mayor's kid from the theater."

Shawna's toes curled inside her sneakers.

*Is that how they see me?*

"Ah, Shawna," RJ said, his mask of congeniality firmly in place when he entered the garden room. "Wonderful to see you. I'm going to make myself a cocktail. Would you ladies care to join me?"

Shawna looked at her phone. It wasn't even noon yet.

"Why not?" Liz replied. "Shawna?"

"Uh, okay."

Shawna thought, here's my chance to drink with the grownups, maybe a morning quaff like a Bloody Mary or a Mimosa.

She wasn't expecting gin martinis.

While Liz licked her lips in anticipation, RJ made an elaborate show of shoving aside a stack of faded Playbills on the coffee table and setting down a silver tray with a shaker, a stirrer, and a dish of olives.

The first two rounds of drinks were pleasant enough, with both RJ and Liz entertaining Shawna with remembrances of productions past, even acting out some of the anecdotes, including the time a deer crashed through an open exit door and made it onto the stage. But by the third round of martinis, Shawna realized her error in drinking with the Jennings, especially when RJ began ranting about the theater and how the board fired him when it was Wick's fault all along.

Shawna wasn't quite sure how Dudley Wicks caused RJ to make an ass of himself at the General Greene Inn or crash his car, but he was sticking to that narrative. Wicks, RJ insisted with slurring speech, was trying to sabotage the theater because he knew his play was a turkey and it was too late to pull out. Equally drunk, Liz nodded in agreement so aggressively her seashell earrings danced.

Shawna, recalling how Liz had declared Wick's adaptation "genius," was confused. And throwing away her journalistic instincts during the boozy afternoon, she'd neglected to inquire about Liz's change of attitude.

"The only way he can get out of our contract is by a force majeure," RJ slurred before mixing more martinis.

In her clouded brain, Shawna recalled that term meant *Act of God*. Would a fire fit the bill? Would Wicks put the company's lives at risk just to cover his interests?

They both asserted that Dudley Wicks should be arrested for manslaughter, but the coward had fled to New York.

"If you ask me, Wicks is in cahoots with the power players of this town," Liz said, perhaps forgetting who Shawna's father was. "They all want the theater destroyed so they can build their damn housing development."

"Over my dead body!" boomed RJ, his face reddening.

"You always say that, RJ!" Liz screeched. "And nothing ever changes."

"Will you stop busting my balls!" RJ rammed his fist into the coffee table, upsetting the tray of olives.

"Now, look what you did," Liz whined and reached for a tissue box to mop up the mess.

Feeling increasingly like she was trapped in a nightmarish production of *Who's Afraid of Virginia Woolf*, Shawna excused herself and headed for the door, leaving *Martha* and *George* to fight it out. She doubted if they even noticed that she had left.

Later, safely home but still feeling the effects of the martinis, Shawna lay on her bed and tried to stop the room from spinning. She had been drunk before at college parties but never like this. She tried to recall how many drinks she'd consumed. Was it four? Five?

Just thinking about it made her--

Unable to tamp down the rising tide of nausea, Shawna hopped off the bed, bolted to her bathroom, and lifted the toilet seat just in time. She remained on the floor until her stomach was empty and raw, then crawled, humiliated, back to bed.

*How anyone can drink this stuff and like it is beyond me. Never again!*

## CHAPTER 12

The first rehearsal had just resumed after the two-week break, when Liz crashed through the double doors at the back of the house shouting, "RJ, the masks are gone!"

RJ twisted irritably in his seat from the front row and glared at his wife. "Can't you see we're working?"

Penny stopped in the middle of a dance routine and mopped her face with the towel draped around her neck. Rex cursed under his breath at the interruption.

"This is important," panted Liz as she strutted down the center aisle to approach RJ. "The award from Mayor Bill. You know, the comedy and tragedy masks?"

"Yes, what about them?"

"Well, they were in the trophy case, and now they're gone." Liz's face was flushed from the effort of walking.

"Alright," groaned RJ. "Everyone take ten."

"Ten minutes," Blake announced grumpily.

Shawna took the opportunity during the break to fill up her water bottle. Gazing up at the catwalk, Shawna could see the new LED lights that had been installed. Somehow, the town council had come up with the money to pay for it, which explained why her Dad had been in a foul mood ever since.

Complicating matters was that Wicks' lawyer had sent a registered letter to the theater demanding payment for the entire season, plus extra for pain and suffering and the relinquishment of the rights to his musical. However, the contract Wicks signed, RJ insisted, was ironclad, giving the theater first rights to mount the show, regardless of Wicks' participation. Shawna was impressed with RJ's role as not only a great artist but also an eagle-eyed negotiator. Besides, Ron and Harriet were in charge of that department; RJ relied on their expertise to handle it.

"I think one of the electrician helpers must have stolen the masks," Liz said. "Do you know some of these hooligans steal the copper from our town's streetlights and air conditioning units?"

"Who cares about the goddamn masks?" hissed RJ. "We're already weeks behind and can't have any more of these silly interruptions."

"All right," Liz said with pursed lips. "But that case will look awfully empty come opening night."

Shawna could see that RJ was close to losing it. She wondered about the state of the Jennings' marriage.

"The town council can get us new masks by then. Now, can we please get on with it!" RJ stood and drove his fist into the stage's apron, a reprise of his gesture used to great effect during his performance as Willy Loman in *Death of a Salesman*.

Shawna was glad when the rehearsal started up again. She didn't believe that her Dad would ever commission another award, but she kept it to herself. He was in no mood to spend any more of the town's budget on what he considered a "money-draining eyesore."

Pressed for lost time, the demands on the company were enormous; everyone was feeling the heat. The cast had to relearn what they'd forgotten during the two-week interim, especially Penny, who seemed to be starting from scratch. The stress on Rex's face was apparent while he patiently retaught her the dance moves.

After a particularly challenging day, the cast unwound at the usual spot. While RJ pounded out another show tune on the piano, Shawna just happened to glance out the window in time to see Dudley Wicks drive past in his sky-blue antique Mercedes convertible. He was heading toward the theater.

Shawna wondered if Wicks had stolen the comedy and tragedy masks just to be petty. She glanced around the bar, wondering if she should alert anyone to Wick's presence, but recalling her Dad's words about never stirring the pot, she quickly decided against it. Wicks could have an excellent reason for driving through town. Perhaps he was still moving out of his rental. Blake, who'd stayed behind to help hang lights, would be there to confront him if he did show up at the theater.

Besides, Shawna thought, listening to Liz belt out *Some People* from *Gypsy*, everyone was having such a good time--everyone except Penny.

Scanning the bar, Shawna noticed the bottle blonde sitting alone in the corner booth sucking down a drink. Above the lip of her cocktail glass, Penny glared at Shawna with unveiled malice.

∽

"Did you know the masks you gave the theater are missing?" Shawna asked her Dad that evening over dinner.

Bill had just removed the steaks from the outdoor grill.

"Are you serious?" replied Bill, obviously annoyed. "Who would do such a thing?"

Shawna tried not to think of Dougal's face when she cut into her medium-rare steak. Her Dad had the chef's snobby habit of undercooking meat. "Liz thought one of the workers stole it for the metal. Were they made out of copper or something?"

Bill laughed. "No, silly. It was just a cheap polymer made to look like bronze."

"Oh, so it wouldn't cost much to replace it?"

"Well." Bill cut into his own steak and took a pleasing bite. "I have more important things to worry about, like figuring out how I'm going to balance the budget after we had to replace those damn school buses."

The town's budgetary issues bored her, but Shawna kept up a good pretense of listening while she mulled over the scenes she had worked on that day. Feeling more and more confident in her role as understudy, she was required to learn Liz's role as well, although she couldn't imagine playing Clytemnestra. Besides, Liz had famously never missed a performance in all her years at the theater.

Penny was another matter. She seemed to be struggling in her role as Cassandra more and more, especially during her big solo number at the end of Act One when Agamemnon brings Cassandra back to his palace as a spoil of the Trojan War. As Cassandra approaches the palace doors, she knows the vengeful queen, Clytemnestra, will murder her. Horrified, Cassandra can see her fate and that of the king, but she knows that no one will believe her prophecy because of the curse placed on her by Apollo. The solo song was written as a showstopper, but Penny's tone-deaf delivery and awkward movements were making a mockery of it.

To cover Penny's limitations in the dance department, Rex had devised clever choreography for a small chorus of taunting Harpies to cavort around the stage during the number. But even the most impressive moves and sophisticated lighting effects could not compensate for Penny's flat voice and lack of emotional depth.

During the last run-through of the number, even Katie Higgins, the nicest girl in the show, had rolled her eyes and mumbled, "She sucks," under her breath. Shawna fought hard not to laugh. When Blake called for a break, not even a skilled Thespian like RJ could hide his disappointment.

Later, as Shawna was heading out the door, tired from a long day of rehearsal and looking forward to an evening dip in the pool, she overheard RJ and Liz having a heated discussion in the women's dressing room.

"Why don't you fire her and put the juvenile in?"

It took Shawna a moment to realize Liz was talking about her.

"I'm not going to fire Penny. Are you mad?" boomed RJ to his wife. "She's the most popular actress in the company...excluding you, of course."

*Nice save, RJ*, Shawna noted.

"Perhaps she was miscast," RJ suggested.

"Ya think?" squawked Liz.

"I'll work with Penny privately."

Liz's intake of breath could be heard through the door. "Oh, I bet you'll work with her privately. I'm not falling for that again."

"And I'm not falling for your jealous suspicions! All I

care about is this theater. I can't afford a flop with everything that's happened!"

"So fire Penny and put the kid in!"

"I'll think about it, Liz. But this is the last time I want to discuss it. Don't you understand what kind of pressure I'm under?"

Shawna escaped down the corridor as RJ flung open the dressing room door to leave.

About to head outside, Shawna recalled Judith's request that she retrieve the costumes she had left in the hayloft during the horrible accident. She thought that maybe she should just get them now and be done with it. She was sweaty anyway. She'd do the right thing, delay gratification for her nightly swim, and prove to the company that she was still a trooper despite her elevated understudy status.

Satisfied with her plan, Shawna continued into the bowels of the barn where old scenery and stage lights were stored, wondering if she would run into Harriet again. Shawna had meant to ask Judith if this area was a shortcut to Harriet's office because she couldn't imagine why anyone in a wheelchair would traverse through such a dusty maze. She realized she hadn't quite learned the old barn's many twists and turns.

Shawna reached the *Gypsy* cow and was about to rub its nose for good luck when a flash of light near the old, rusted metal cow cages caught her eye.

"Hello?" Shawna said, craning her neck to peer into the darkness. All was quiet.

*It must be just a flare from a window or something.*

But there were no windows at that end of the barn. She was about to place her foot on the ladder's first rung when the sound of rapid footsteps, like someone or something scampering in the shallow distance, broke through the stillness.

"Hey!" she called. "Judith? Harriet, is that you?"

No answer.

Shawna's rational mind told her it was an old barn, and field mice were a constant annoyance. Recalling RJ's deer story, she hoped it wasn't a larger animal trapped inside: a raccoon or something.

But hadn't Judith just told her the exterminator had given the place a good once over when the electricity was being overhauled? She stood frozen for a moment, wondering if she should climb the ladder or save the task for the following day, when the metallic flash revealed itself to be much more than just an optical illusion or the figment of a fertile imagination.

Shawna sucked in a quick breath; her heart fluttered with fear. At the end of the dark corridor was a figure wearing one of the long gauzy harpy tunics she'd hung up in the chorus's dressing room only the day before. Obscuring the figure's face was the missing tragedy mask. The mask's exaggerated features gave the moving figure a ghoulishly large head.

Frozen in fear, Shawna watched the figure move toward her, seeming to float in its flowing tunic. Malevolence glinted behind the mask's eyeholes as the figure lifted its arm to reveal a large knife.

Jolted into action, Shawna turned and ran, but in her haste she stumbled over her own feet and crashed to the ground. The rough-hewn floorboards rose to meet her, driving a splinter into her shin. Shawna screamed from pain and terror as the figure lunged at her.

Rolling onto her back, she kicked at the figure's midsection, causing it to stumble backwards. But it quickly recovered its footing and vaulted forward for another attack. Shawna grappled desperately with her attacker. The knife stabbed the air mere inches from her throat. Shawna grabbed hold of the figure's wrist, twisting it till the knife clattered to the floor.

Shawna grunted, "Get the fuck off me!"

Grabbing onto the mask, she landed a solid knee into the figure's gut. With a groan, it finally toppled off her. Shawna scrambled to her feet, still holding the mask. Her attacker lay on the floor in a sea of black gauze, propped up on its elbows, and breathing heavily. Shawna stared in disbelief at the red, angry face surrounded by disheveled blond locks.

"Penny!"

## CHAPTER 13

"What the hell is going on here?"

Shawna turned to see Hutch jogging toward them.

"Shawna, are you all right?"

Penny had already gotten to her feet and was pulling the gauzy tunic over her head. She tossed it aside irritably. Appearing harmless as ever in her hot pink bike shorts and rainbow print crop top, she raked her fingers through her damp hair and said, "Of course, she's all right. For chrissakes, I was fooling around. What's the matter, Shawna? Can't you handle a little backstage prank?"

"It's not funny!" Shawna shouted, halfway between anger and tears.

Hutch took the tragedy mask from Shawna's hand and shook his head with disgust. "Penny, Shawna's right. It's not funny. Look, she hurt her leg."

Shawna's knee was bleeding where the splinter had punctured her flesh.

"It's not my fault she's clumsy," said Penny.

Still shaking, Shawna picked up the knife and showed it to Hutch. "S-she tried to stab me with this."

Penny burst out laughing when the knife wobbled in Shawna's grip. "Haven't you ever seen a prop knife before? Boy, you are a green one, aren't you?"

"All right, Penny," said Hutch. "That's enough."

"You know, Shawna," Penny said in a voice dripping with condescension, "We all have to go through a sort of initiation to be part of this theater. We've all had pranks played on us. Isn't that right, Hutch?"

Hutch gazed disapprovingly at Penny. "Yes, but she's just a kid."

"I was just a kid when you and Rex locked me in the cow cage and then went to dinner without me. I was screaming my head off and scared shitless, but I laughed about it later. We all laughed about it." She slid a narrowed gaze at Shawna. "You need to grow a backbone, or you'll never become an actress."

Hutch crouched down a bit so that he was eye level with Shawna. Never had she felt like more like a child. "It was a joke, Shawna. I'm sorry if you hurt yourself, and so is Penny."

Not ready to relinquish her outrage, Shawna pointed at the tragedy mask. "She stole that mask from the display case."

Hutch looked at Penny with raised eyebrows.

"I didn't steal the damn thing! I found it on the prop table. Maybe you'd better stop making up stories, Shawna."

"And maybe you'd better stop lying!"

Hutch wedged himself between the warring women and said, "That's enough out of both of you."

Shawna was about to yell out how she hadn't done anything wrong, how it was all Penny's fault, but the words died on her lips when she realized it would only make her seem even more childish in Hutch's eyes. Her cheeks burned at the injustice of it all.

Hutch turned the mask over in his hands. "I'll make sure this gets returned to the display case. Hopefully, the other one will turn up too." He smiled at Shawna. "It's been a long day. Whatever you were doing back here can wait till tomorrow."

"Fine," Shawna said. She turned on her heels and headed toward the dressing rooms, with as much dignity as she could muster, limping slightly from the pain in her leg. She hated being dismissed this way, but she was powerless. Penny was clearly in the wrong. A harmless prank is one thing, but the rage glimmering in Penny's eyes and the aggression of the attack were real. Shawna didn't believe the ruse about the mask being on the prop table, either. She'd passed that prop table at least a dozen times that day and would have surely noticed it.

More incensed with each hobbled step, Shawna made her way to the women's dressing room to pick up her things and get the hell out of there.

As she swung open the door, a sharp gasp escaped her lips at the sight of a mysterious figure nestled in the corner chair. Her alarm faded as she realized it was the dummy she'd often seen at various locations backstage. Bald, naked, and resembling an oversized stuffed doll, the dummy was harmless. Still, it rattled Shawna.

*More of Penny's tricks?*

Shawna picked up the dummy and plopped it into Penny's seat at the makeup table just to mess with her.

*Two can play at this game.*

She left the theater through one of the side doors.

Fuming mad, she mounted her bike and checked for any

oncoming cars before crossing the two-lane highway. She felt shaky riding home, her emotions alternating between anger and embarrassment. She parked her bike in the garage beside the Lexus and limped into the house. When she passed her Dad at the stove, she burst into tears.

"Hey, honey," he said, lowering the flame on a saucepan. "What's wrong?" He followed her into the family room.

Shawna plopped down on the couch. "I fell off my bike," she said, feeling about five years old. She didn't want to lie to her Dad, but she didn't want to be seen as a baby either. She wanted him to believe she could handle anything, even nasty pranks like the one Penny had just pulled on her.

Bill's brow wrinkled with concern. "Are you okay?"

"I'm okay, but I think I got a splinter."

"I'll get the tweezers."

She leaned her head back on the soft sofa cushions, recalling what it was like when her Mom cared for her cuts and scrapes and made everything better.

Bill returned with the tweezers, tilted the shade of the reading lamp for a better look, and painlessly removed the splinter.

Bill held the splinter up the light. "That's some plank you got there. You said you got this from falling on the road?"

"Yeah, there was a branch down or something."

He looked at her skeptically, but let it go.

Shawna was afraid that if she told him the real story, he'd have even more reason to hate the theater, and she was determined not only to finish out the season, but to finish it victoriously and enact her revenge. If anyone deserved a little payback, it was Penny McNeil.

## CHAPTER 14

The following day's rehearsal focused on the pivotal scene where Clytemnestra murders Agamemnon and Cassandra. In the original Greek play, the violence happens offstage, and the bloody aftermath is revealed in a theatrical tableau, but RJ knew offstage didn't fill seats. A bloodbath would repel the theater's mostly elderly audience, but a highly stylized dance number would dramatize the moment within the limits of good taste. Liz was far past her dancing days, but Rex's clever choreography concealed her limitations. While waiting for the chorus members to be added to the dance, Shawna watched from the wings with bated breath. This was only a rehearsal, and already she was feeling the catharsis of witnessing Clytemnestra's revenge, especially with Penny playing the victim role.

Penny appeared more subdued than usual. Perhaps Hutch had had a stern "talk" with her about her behavior the night before. Shawna preferred a low-keyed Penny backstage, but her role as the prophetess Cassandra called for deep emotions, which Penny lacked. When Liz, as Clytemnestra, play-stabbed her with the same wobbly prop knife Penny had wielded against Shawna, RJ stopped the action. Blake killed the music track. Everyone froze and looked at RJ, who stood in the front row, rubbing his eyes.

"Penny, you need to give me more of a reaction." He stopped rubbing his eyes and glared at her. "I don't even know what you're playing here."

Penny stammered. "I-I'm playing fear. I'm playing terror."

"That's terror?" RJ tried to control the sarcasm in his tone, but it spilled out regardless. "I show more terror when I open the morning paper."

Liz burst out laughing. "It's true. He does." Her attempt to lighten the mood fell flat. All the actors on stage looked uncomfortably toward Penny or at the floor.

"Just tell me what you want me to do, and I'll do it." Penny's voice squeaked.

RJ shook his head sadly as if she were a lost cause. "Take ten. Except Rex. I need to talk to you."

"Ten minutes!" Blake shouted.

"Thank you, ten," chorused back the company except for Penny, who appeared visibly deflated.

"Hey, Shawna. Hope you're feeling better today."

Shawna spun to see a smiling Hutch heading toward her.

"Thanks. I'm okay," she said. "I've never seen RJ so upset."

Hutch shrugged. "I'm sure it will all work out." His smile dropped when he spotted Penny approaching. "I'll see you later, Shawna."

Penny shouldered her as she passed.

"Hey," Shawna blurted. She was about to tell Penny off when Hutch gave her a pleading look as he led Penny away.

Liz shuffled by and gave Shawna's arm a light pat before retiring to the dressing room for a quick rest between scenes. Liz's deep sigh seemed to indicate there were problems with the show. It was sad to see the energy drop when everyone was on fire before, everyone except Penny. She was so obviously the weak link in the chain, the cog gumming up the works. To avoid any more drama, Shawna crossed the stage. She paused when she passed RJ and Rex who were deep in conversation.

"That's a brilliant idea," RJ said, excitedly clasping Rex's arm. "It will take some of the focus off Cassandra during that scene."

Rex beamed in the warmth of RJ's praise. "My grandma always said, 'You can't make chicken salad out of chicken shit,' but this might just work."

RJ rolled his head back and laugh.

Shawna marveled at how theater people could be down one moment and inspired the next. As she sallied to the water fountain to refill her bottle, she hummed the old Ethel Merman standard: *There's no people like show people. They smile when they are low.*

～

After the break, RJ assembled the cast and explained that he cut the massacre scene.

"What?" cried Penny.

"The most violent acts in the Greek theater happened offstage," he pedantically explained. "This new concept will be an homage to that tradition. The audience's imagination will fill in the blanks, leave them wanting more."

Penny's pink lips made an outraged O. She glanced at Hutch, who wouldn't meet her eyes.

To Shawna's ears, it sounded like a silly rationalization to hide Penny's bad acting during the most critical scene in the play. But if it kept Penny's lousy performance from spoiling the show, she fully supported the decision. Shawna also suspected that RJ cut the scene because Bob, the older gentleman from the chorus, just didn't have the physique to pull off the role of Aegisthus, Clytemnestra's lover and partner in crime. As a result, the character was cut from the script and only mentioned in the finale. Shawna thought it was a good solution to an obvious problem, but she wondered what Wicks would think of RJ butchering his masterpiece.

Inspired by this new concept, RJ's hands drew pictures in the air as he described the scene in full, dramatic detail.

"Clytemnestra will still be down center," RJ said.

"Damn straight," mumbled Liz.

"Cassandra will be here, already dead." RJ pointed to a spot behind Liz's position. He thought for a moment before scanning the chorus. "Katie, you will play Cassandra."

Katie jumped up and clapped. "Sure, I'll play dead for you."

Shawna found Katie's positive attitude refreshing.

*That's exactly the energy we need at this moment.*

RJ circled the company until he stood center stage. "And here, we'll add a flashback sequence."

"Flashback sequence!" cried Penny. "That's not in the script."

"No, it's not," replied RJ gravely. "But since when does this theater play by the rules?"

Shawna saw what RJ was doing and was impressed. By pretending this was the bold move by an innovative director instead of clumsy stagecraft to cover a sub-par performance, RJ was saving face while strategically bolstering the company's morale. It's the kind of strategy, that ability to think of one's feet, which sets a creative artist apart from the rest.

"The flashback sequence will be played right here." RJ made an expansive gesture with his arms.

"Flashback of what?" asked Penny, her voice flat, uninspired.

"Iphigenia's sacrifice!"

The company stared back blankly, cueing Shawna that no one had researched the original myth. Actors were known to be lazy and to read only their "sides." But Shawna had studied the play in her classic literature course. She knew that Iphigenia was Cassandra and Agamemnon's daughter, whom Agamemnon had sacrificed to achieve victory at Troy. This bloody deed forms the basis for Clytemnestra's revenge, not only her jealousy over Cassandra.

RJ looked at Shawna and held out his hand. "And Shawna, you will play Iphigenia."

Shawna looked around. "Me?"

"Yes, you," RJ said.

Shawna nervously stepped forward and took RJ's hand.

Hutch looked confused, "But how can I be dead and do the sacrifice?"

RJ brushed the question away with his hand. "We'll use one of the other actors or a dummy if we have to."

"I'll do it," said Bob. "I played a great dummy on Broadway."

Everyone laughed at Bob's joke except Penny.

"Are you seriously going to put her center stage during this scene?" asked Penny, pointing at Shawna.

RJ stood his ground. "Yes. Is there a problem?"

"Uh, you seemed to have forgotten that she's the understudy. What if one of us gets sick?"

"Fat chance," huffed Liz. "I've never missed a performance in my career."

RJ's lips tightened. "Well, stay healthy and make sure you don't get sick. All right!" He clapped his hands together. "Let's block this scene and then break for lunch."

## CHAPTER 15

Shawna realized how lucky she was to have an opportunity to be featured in a scene, much less *the* scene, even though she had no lines to recite. The entire sequence depended on movement, and RJ instructed Rex to choreograph it like a dance, counting out each beat. The scene required a company member to drag Shawna onstage to the sacrificial stone. Jim Connelly, a pimply-faced fourteen-year-old kid from her neighborhood, was recruited for the task. At five feet six and one-twenty pounds, Jim looked like he could barely drag a cat. Shawna realized it would require a lot of acting to pull it off, but she was ready to try her best.

Using stage combat techniques, Rex showed Shawna how to play-resist being dragged so she didn't hurt herself. The first time they rehearsed it, Jim pressed his fingers so hard into her upper arms she squealed, forcing RJ to halt the rehearsal. They got the hang of it after a few tries and a stiff warning from Blake for Jim to take it easy. RJ stopped the rehearsal while this complex piece of stage business was discussed and reworked. While the company relaxed, Shawna felt the weight of Penny's hateful glare.

*It's not my fault you suck*, Shawna thought, tossing her red curls over her shoulder to show Penny she wasn't afraid of her.

When the company broke for lunch, Shawna decided to eat outdoors in the sunshine. She had just found a shady spot beneath the willow tree adjacent to the parking lot when Penny plopped beside her cross-legged on the grass.

"Penny, I--"

"Listen, bitch, and listen good." Penny's face was so close to hers that Shawna could see the fine vertical lines fanning across her lips, probably from smoking too much. Her breath smelled of nicotine and Trident. Her raised finger pointed knife-like at Shawna's throat. "Don't think I don't know what you're doing. And you're not going to get away with it."

Determined to show no fear, Shawna stared down Penny's finger, daring her to move it any closer. "I don't know what you're talking about. RJ gave me the role. If you don't like it, take it up with him."

"Oh, I will, don't worry." Penny stood and wiped the loose grass from the seat of her *Daisy Dukes*. "I'm going to speak to RJ right now."

"You do that," replied Shawna to Penny's retreating ass.

Shawna didn't know where she found the grit to stick up for herself, but she was glad she did. Unfortunately, the encounter had an unsettling effect on her stomach, and she lost her appetite. She put her lunch back into the brown paper bag and spent the rest of the break lounging on the grass, imagining sacrificing Penny in ways appropriate for Greek tragedy; except in her fantasies, she didn't use a prop knife.

The afternoon was spent on Hutch's solo, so Blake sent the rest of the cast home. Shawna was in the women's dressing room gathering her things when Judith reminded her, not so tactfully, that her first duty as an intern was helping out backstage and that there was still plenty of work to do. Shawna wasn't so sure if that applied anymore. After all, her participation on stage earned her Equity points, but she decided against arguing. Having one company member hating her was enough for one season.

Determined to prove she was still a "trooper" despite her newly elevated position, Shawna returned reluctantly to the hayloft to complete the task. It was a dirty job; the hayloft was hot and stuffy. After climbing the ladder, Shawna loaded the costumes into black trash bags and tossed them out of the hayloft door onto the parking lot. From there, she could load them through the back door near the dressing rooms.

While dragging the last bag through the backdoor, Shawna almost locked herself out when she mistakenly kicked the paint can out of the way.

*Someone really needs to fix that damn lock*, she grumbled. She was surprised that had gotten past the Fire Marshall's inspection. But she wasn't going to be the one who blew the whistle. The last thing the theater needed was another delay.

Once Shawna had hung up each tunic and robe in the women's dressing room that doubled as Judith's workspace, she saw how dirty and stiff they were. When Shawna realized the white marks on one of the tunics that she was steaming were pigeon droppings, she stepped back with disgust. "Judith, these are gross. Can't we get new costumes for the production?"

"Who's going to build them? You?" Judith hissed, her

front teeth clamping down on a pin.

"Well, can we wash them at least?"

Judith removed the pin from her mouth and stabbed it into the costume on the dress form, thought for a moment and said, "There's a washer and dryer in the basement. Some volunteers donated it years ago. It was a real bitch to hook up, let me tell you."

"Basement? I didn't know this old barn had a basement."

"Sure does, but the ceilings are really low, so watch your head when you're going down."

"Okay. How do I get there?"

Judith took a deep breath, and Shawna braced herself for what she knew would be a long and complicated series of directions.

"Here's what you do," Judith began. "You know where the cow cages are?"

"Yeah."

"Ignore them. Pretend like they don't exist."

"Okay."

"You're going to go in the other direction till you reach the lobby."

"Where the gala was held?"

"Yeah. You know what a lobby is, don't you?"

"Uh-huh."

"You're going to go through the lobby," Judith continued.

"So, don't ignore it." Shawna couldn't help herself.

"Right. Don't ignore it."

"Okay. Got it."

"Go inside the box office."

"Uh-huh."

"Inside the box office is a tiny door." Judith indicated about five feet off the ground. "That's the door to the basement. The light switch is on your left. You'll find the washing machine unit, along with old props and stuff down there."

Shawna scooped up an armful of the nastiest costumes and made her way to the lobby as per Judith's instructions. The theater was quiet. She wondered if Hutch had left already. When she arrived at the box office, she discovered that the door to the basement was even smaller than Judith's description. It appeared like a door in *Alice in Wonderland* after Alice grew big. She wondered how on earth anyone squeezed a washer and dryer through the opening.

The door stuck when she tried to open it. At last, she found success after a few good yanks. But just as she ducked down to pass through the door, she heard someone enter the lobby. Peeking her head above the box office counter, she spotted Rex with his phone plastered to his ear.

"He's stealing all my ideas and not giving me any of the credit," Rex said in an irritable voice uncharacteristic of the man Shawna had gotten to know. "He sent everyone home early. He's probably getting drunk at the bar. What the hell did I get myself into?"

There was silence while Rex stopped and listened to the voice on the other end.

"Okay. I'll look for it and let you know. But promise you'll be here for final dress."

Shawna tried not to breathe while Rex listened for a moment.

"Well, sneak in if you have to," Rex responded to whomever was speaking. "I need you here. Also, this place is giving me the creeps. After what happened to the TD, they should have shut down this rattrap. You wouldn't believe the idiots they have me working with."

Shawna's cheeks burned. She hoped Rex wasn't talking

about her. There were worse idiots in the cast, Penny, for one.

Rex laughed uproariously at whatever was said on the other end. "Okay, babe. I'll try. I'm going to look for it now. I'll text you if I find anything. Ciao."

Shawna waited, frozen, taking only tiny breaths until she was sure Rex had left the lobby. She thought Rex was happy here. He certainly acted the part. She gazed down the rickety and worn wooden steps descending into the basement's total blackness and felt sadness wash over her. She'd have never guessed Rex to be so duplicitous.

*I guess everyone wears a mask in real life. Isn't that what the theater's for? To reveal truths we cannot comprehend in our regular, everyday lives?*

After fumbling for the light switch along the dusty walls, she located a string dangling from the ceiling and yanked it. The fluorescent lights flickered to life, casting an eerie greenish glow on the faded plaster walls.

Shawna slowly descended the open-tread staircase, noting an unpleasant cat urine odor among the general mustiness. At least, she hoped it was from a stray cat and not a raccoon or, God forbid, a skunk. As she reached the halfway point on the stairs, she became convinced that she heard movement in the dark recesses of the space.

What was worse, she wondered – bird poop on costumes or a stray cat in the basement? After careful consideration, she concluded that no one should go on stage in a dirty costume.

Each stair creaked with protest until she landed on the damp concrete floor. Like the attic, the basement stretched to dark infinity in every direction. It didn't take her long to spot the washer/dryer. Next to the unit was another set of stairs leading to a double hurricane door canopied with cobwebs.

*So, that's how they hauled the washer and dryer down here.*

Feeling a bit more comfortable with the lay of the land, Shawna loaded the costumes into the washing machine. A 70s-styled housewife grinned at her from a box of detergent beneath layers of dust. It was apparent Judith hadn't washed a costume in many seasons. Shawna shook some detergent from the box, closed the washing machine lid, dialed to the proper setting, and--hoping for the best--pressed the start button. She waited, for what seemed like an eternity, for the machine to engage. When she heard the water groaning through the rusty pipes, she sighed with relief.

*I'll let the cycle run through and return tomorrow to load the dryer.*

Eager to leave the somber place, she turned her back on the washing machine and moved quickly toward the staircase. A scurrying noise stopped her dead in her tracks.

The only other sounds were the washing machine's whirl and the fluorescent light's buzz.

Shawna recalled how her Dad once told her to always trust her instincts as far as danger was concerned, that women, especially, had a keen inner alarm system to which they should always yield.

Shawna considered that now as a tingling sensation began at the nape of her neck and radiated through her hair follicles.

Taking her Dad's advice, she ran for the stairs, bounding up two steps at a time as if hellhounds were nipping at her heels. But another instinct, curiosity, made her stop halfway up the stairs. Through the stairs' open treads, she observed a rumpled blanket, a box of Ritz Crackers, and a jar of peanut butter on the floor. It seemed someone had been napping and snacking beneath the stairs. Had the items been left for some animal?

Shawna continued up the stairs without pausing to investigate any further and made for the door. But as she crouched to pass through, it slammed in her face.

## CHAPTER 16

Shawna's scalp burned. Sweat beaded her forehead.
*Be calm*, she told herself. *It was probably just a draft. Old barns are drafty. Remember?*

She reached out, fumbled with the doorknob, twisted it, and pushed forward.

*Stuck! The door's stuck! But it stuck before. Push it harder!*

She tried again with a bit more force. The old glass knob spun in her sweaty palm. The door wouldn't budge.

"Hey!" she yelled, driving her fist into the scarred wood. When the echo of her banging faded, a rustling sound rose from the basement floor below her. Flushed with panic, she lunged forward, striking the door with her shoulder.

The door still wouldn't yield. Her shoulder flamed. She rubbed it, concerned she might have torn something. But physical injury was a small price to pay for escaping whatever was making its presence known in the dungeon below.

She stood silently at the top of the stairs, hands pressed into the rough plaster walls on either side of the narrow stairs, deciding what to do next. She also listened and hoped that the noise she heard was all in her mind. She was tired.

It was a long day, and she was alone in a creepy place. Of course, her imagination would get the best of her. And if she did hear something, it was probably a mouse, a squirrel, or, at worst, a raccoon or stray cat--all harmless. Then she recalled the makeshift bed beneath the stairs, the crackers and peanut butter, the crumbs sprinkled about. That detritus could only be from a human, but what kind of maniac would camp out down there?

The disturbing thought stirred her to action. Rex had been in the lobby just a minute ago. Perhaps he hadn't left the theater yet.

"Rex!" she screamed as she pounded against the door. "I'm locked in the basement! Rex! Is anybody there? Please, help!"

She banged a few more times, with increased force, until her wrist bent back with a flash of pain. She laid two hard kicks against the wood, thinking she might break through one of the door panels, but she almost broke her toe in the process.

Her knees buckled, and she sank to the top step, gripping her aching foot.

*There has to be another way out of here. Maybe if I keep exploring the basement, I'll find another staircase.*

But walking alone into the darkness with no light source seemed like a last-ditch effort at best. She tapped each pocket of her shorts, hoping her phone was in one of them and not in her backpack in the dressing room where she'd left it. The washing machine clicked and then whirred into a spin as it entered another cycle.

As she remembered the hurricane doors, her heart filled with hope--a path to freedom! With renewed confidence, she stood and started down the stairs, ignoring the dark shadows creeping into her peripheral vision.

Halfway down, a hand emerged between the treads of the stairs and grabbed her ankle, gripping it tightly.

Shawna screamed. She struggled to yank her foot loose, but the icy grip only tightened. The hand was strong, upsetting Shawna's balance. She began to fall forward, and it seemed to her as if everything happened in slow motion. None of it seemed real. She imagined that RJ would enter the scene at any moment and tell her to try a different approach, that she was acting the scene all wrong. She was experiencing an actor's nightmare and would wake up any second. But there was nothing make-believe about the way her teeth rattled in her head when she crashed on the hard concrete. Now she understood what it meant in cartoons when characters saw stars because she was seeing them now.

The room plunged into darkness before a flash of light illuminated a figure in a flowing black hooded robe crouching over her, but this time the comedy mask, frozen in a hideous laugh, was affixed to its face. A large knife hung in the air for a moment before hurtling down with the swiftness of a guillotine's blade. Shawna rolled away just in time. The knife's point struck the concrete floor, skidded and sparked.

*That knife is no prop!*

Shawna crab-crawled backward shouting, "Penny! Stop! This isn't funny!"

The caped figure lunged at her again. Shawna lifted her knees to her chest and mule-kicked it square in the chest. The figure stumbled back and fell. Shawna jumped to her feet and dashed toward the hurricane doors. Clawing through cobwebs, she thrust her shoulder against the wood. The heavy doors gave a little, letting in a blast of cool air.

"Please! Please!"

The masked figure slowly got to its feet and began moving toward Shawna, teasingly weaving the knife through the air.

"Penny! Stop it!" Shawna screamed, slamming all of her weight into the double doors.

The mask tilted to one side, the exaggerated mouth and eyes holes catching grotesque shadows.

Grunting and groaning, Shawna pushed on the doors, but they wouldn't open all the way.

"Penny, why are you doing this?"

Wild eyes glinted behind the holes in the mask.

"You're insane!" Shawna screamed, kicking out her feet as the figure slowly approached.

A flash of light appeared at the top of the stairs.

"Hey! Is anyone there?" a voice called down the basement stairs.

The figure turned, and Shawna burst forward. Pushing her attacker aside, Shawna flew up the stairs and, in her haste, banged her head hard on the low doorjamb.

Everything went black.

She awoke on one of the lobby's benches wrapped in Hutch's arms.

"Shawna," he said, brushing loose strands of hair from her damp face. "Are you alright?"

"Y-yeah. I'm okay. I think." Her head pounded when she sat up. She felt slightly nauseous.

"What were you doing down there?"

"I-I was doing laundry." It sounded ridiculous and horrifying all at once. She began to sob.

"Now, now." Hutch gently rubbed the sore spot right below the hairline. "Sheesh. You gave yourself a real goose egg running up those stairs." He gently sat her upright. "I'll get you an ice pack. Blake keeps a supply in the fridge."

"No!" Shawna cried, gripping his arm. "Don't leave me alone."

"Hey. You really got spooked down there. Someone should have told you that old door sticks. Just one of many things that need fixing in this old barn."

"Penny just tried to kill me," Shawna croaked.

Hutch laughed. "What are you talking about? You mean that prank she tried to play on you the other night?"

"No! Just now." Shawna pointed a trembling finger at the box office door. "She's dressed up in a cape and mask again, and she tried to stab me with a knife. A real knife, this time."

Hutch tightened his mouth and shook his head. "Maybe you heard something and thought it was Penny, but--"

"I *know* what I saw. It was Penny. She's fucking crazy!"

Hutch pursed his lips as if shocked by Shawna's language. "Well, I know for a fact that Penny is at the General Greene with RJ and Liz. I only came back because I forgot my script. And I'm glad I did," he gently wiped a tear from Shawna's cheek, "or you might have been here all night imagining all kinds of scary things."

"I didn't imagine it," Shawna said. But the grit had drained from her. She was tired, exhausted, and in pain.

Hutch stood and stretched. "It's getting late." He picked up his script from the bench and tucked it under his arm. "And you, young miss, must get home and put some ice on that bump. You shouldn't be driving either?"

"I-I rode my bike."

Hutch chuckled. "Not tonight. I'll drive you home." He extended his hand and Shawna took it. His large hand nearly swallowed hers, but it was warm and comforting. He flipped off the lobby lights as they made their way out. He checked the door to ensure it was locked and then guided Shawna through the parking lot toward his Jeep Cherokee.

Hutch held the passenger door for her, and she climbed inside.

As soon as he started the ignition, the stereo blasted the Phantom's theme song. He turned down the volume in what Shawna sensed was embarrassment.

After a few moments, Shawna said, "You were great as the Phantom."

Hutch turned to her and beamed.

"You saw that?"

"Three times," Shawna said.

Hutch whistled. "Now, that's the kind of support the theater needs. I don't recall signing your program."

"I was too shy to ask. Ah, turn left at the next stoplight."

"You live in Pennbrook?"

"Yup."

"Nice."

Hutch continued on the road leading to Shawna's development.

He pulled into her driveway, put the jeep in park, and leaned toward her. For a moment she thought he was leaning in for a kiss, but he was only reaching into her seat pocket to retrieve something.

"What's that? A program from Phantom?"

"Yup," Hutch said. "I keep copies of all my programs." He retrieved a pen from the glove compartment. "You know, Shawna." He turned on the interior light and began scribbling on the back of the program. "Sometimes, when I'm having a bad day at the theater, not feeling the role, or doubting myself, I sit in my car and thumb through these old memories." He clicked the pen and handed her the program. "And I remind myself that I have accomplished something in my life. Maybe I'll never make it to Broadway, but I do my best."

The interior light created harsh shadows on Hutch's face, erasing his handsomeness and making him appear almost sinister. Shawna realized she was alone in a vehicle with a man twice her age. She shifted her gaze to her house. Her Dad had left a light on for her. She longed for the comfort of home, her bed, her Dad.

"Thanks for the program," she said, taking it.

Shawna opened the passenger door, and Hutch's smile lit up again, the sinister mask shattered by pearly whites and dimples.

"Anytime," he said. "And don't go down in the basement alone." He waved a paternal finger at her as she climbed out of the car.

"I won't." Before shutting the car door, she leaned in and said. "I appreciate all your help tonight, but it *was* Penny who attacked me. I know it was her, and I know she's your girlfriend and everything--"

He shook his head.

"But she's taking this prank too far. I hate to say it, but she's dangerous."

"But why would she do something like that?"

"Because she hates me. She threatened me yesterday, called me a bitch, and told me to watch out."

Hutch stared straight ahead with a fixed expression on his face.

"I'm sorry if it hurts you, Hutch. But it's the truth."

Hutch smiled, but his eyes were blank, or maybe just tired. "Goodnight, Shawna. Get some rest tonight. And keep an eye on that bump. If you get dizzy or anything, get to the ER. Okay? Do I have to call the Mayor and tell him?"

"No." Shawna sighed. "I'll be fine." She closed the door and waved as Hutch backed out of the driveway, flashing his high beams at her before making the turn.

Later, as she lay in her bed with a melting ice pack on her head and watching shadows dance on her ceiling, she thought about what happened in the basement.

*Hutch didn't believe me. He thinks I'm just some green kid with an overactive imagination.*

Perhaps he really was just a vain actor after all. She switched on the bedside table light and opened the Phantom program to read Hutch's inscription.

*To Shawna, keep your eyes on the stars.*

He'd signed his full name as if his autograph would be worth something someday.

## CHAPTER 17

At breakfast the following day, Bill inquired about how the play was progressing. It was one of the Mayor's rare days off, and he was looking forward to a leisurely morning of golf then lunch at the country club. Shawna had stifled a laugh when he appeared at the table with an overly snug lime green polo shirt and hideous red and green plaid pants. As she crunched on her cornflakes, Shawna contemplated possibly giving Mayor Bill a much-needed makeover, perhaps after the show's opening.

"Rehearsals are going great, Dad." Shawna explained how her part was elevated to the pantomime dance role of the young Cassandra being sacrificed.

Bill raised his eyebrows. "I thought this was a musical?"

"It is, Dad, but it's based on Greek tragedy."

He shook his head and poured more coffee into the silly pink pig mug from their favorite Jersey Shore diner. She hated his disappointed look.

"What's with the face, Dad?"

He shrugged. "I'm not sure how I feel about seeing my daughter sacrificed, even if it's only make-believe."

*Make-believe? He makes it all sound so childish. If only he knew what really went on at the theater--the hard work and dedication, the crazy antics with Penny.*

Although she was still reeling from what had happened in the basement, she couldn't tell her Dad about it. He'd pull her out of the play immediately or maybe even issue an executive order to close the theater down so there could be a full investigation.

"Dad?"

"Yeah, honey?" The morning edition of the Tullytown Times diverted his attention.

"How should you respond to someone you know doesn't like you?"

He gazed at her over the Sports Section. "Someone at the theater?"

"Mm-hmm."

"Who?" His expression was serious.

Sometimes, Shawna wondered if he wasn't too protective of her, especially since her Mom had passed.

Shawna shrugged in an attempt to lighten the mood. "Oh, just that Penny girl. First, she was mad when RJ made me her understudy, and now she's mad that I'm playing Cassandra in the pantomime."

"Jealous," he said, patting her hand. "She's just jealous. Unfortunately, when you stand out in life or show any aptitude or signs of excellence, there's always some idiot on the sidelines criticizing." He refocused on the newspaper.

Shawna wondered if he were speaking about himself. It wasn't easy being a public figure in a small town.

"Also, Dad." Shawna cleared her throat.

"Yeah?" He swung his eyes back to hers.

"Penny played a gag on me the other day. Something

stupid. She said it was part of the theater's hazing ritual and everyone went through it."

She had his full attention now. "What did she do?"

"She dressed up in a costume and tried to stab me with a knife."

"What?" He folded the newspaper and slammed it on the table.

"It was a fake knife, but it kind of scared me. Anyway, it wasn't funny."

Bill shook his head. "It's not funny at all. I'll talk to her."

Shawna flushed. "Who? Penny?"

Bill blinked as if he had been caught doing something wrong. "Yes. Why?"

Shawna shrugged, sensing she and her Dad were drifting into uncomfortable waters. "I just didn't know you knew Penny, outside of seeing her on stage, I mean."

Bill stood with a groan and stretched, revealing a white band of flesh over his waistband. "Some people are always on stage." He gazed down at her with a look of concern tinged with regret. "I don't want my daughter to become one of those silly Thespians."

"Dad, please don't speak to Penny. I'm old enough to handle her myself. I'll tell her today that her behavior is unacceptable, and if he doesn't listen, I'll go to Blake."

"Who's that?"

"The stage manager. She's the first line of defense."

Bill shook his head and brushed off whatever thoughts were brewing there. "Well, I'm going to hit the green before it gets too warm. Need a ride?"

"Nope. I'm good."

Bill looked like he was about to say something else before stopping himself. He turned to fetch his golf clubs from the garage.

Relieved she hadn't divulged too much to her Dad, Shawna rolled her bike out of the driveway behind Bill's Lexus and waved as he drove off.

As Shawna pedaled toward the theater, she rehearsed what she would say to Penny, prepping for every possible parry and counterattack. Her Dad's comments about Penny nettled her, though. Rumors had swirled for years about Penny McNeil's attachment to any number of Tullytown's influential men. Hutch was her long-term boyfriend, but they weren't engaged or even living together. She thought that a bit odd, as they were both in their mid-thirties.

*But then again, theater people.*

While riding her bike to the theater, Shawna dimly recalled a rumor circulating in high school about Penny being the cause of a scandal involving a prominent doctor in town. Dr. Kramer, a well-respected eye surgeon with a private practice in Philadelphia, had left his wife of thirty-five years after his fling with Penny had been discovered. At the time, Penny was moonlighting as a cocktail waitress at the Tullytown Country Club when she apparently caught the aging doctor's eye. The family's twenty-five-year-old daughter discovered Mrs. Kramer hanging in the closet of the master bedroom after receiving an anonymous phone call disclosing the affair. Dr. Kramer left town in disgrace, and their riverfront colonial home was sold. All in all, a family was destroyed by a cheap blonde with no talent--except for the obvious.

A cool breeze lifted Shawna's curls from her damp neck as she coasted downhill toward the familiar red barn. Of course, her Dad knew Penny. Dr. Kramer had once been his good friend and golf buddy. He probably just didn't want to discuss such a lurid topic with his daughter. Mayor Bill was, above all, a skilled diplomat. He'd never tarnish the name of anyone in town, even if they deserved a good tarnishing.

Her bicycle bounced as she trundled over the gravel parking lot. Shawna dismounted and parked in the usual shady spot. Girding her loins for an uncomfortable conversation, Shawna went inside.

"Hey, Penny," Shawna said, entering the women's dressing room. Judith sat squat in the corner, working a needle and thread through the hem of a tunic with a scowl on her face.

"Wassup, bitch?" Penny leaned into the lighted makeup mirror to adjust an errant eyelash.

"I'm not your bitch," Shawna said with as much conviction as she could.

Penny wheeled in her chair, her bleached hair fanning about her face. "I call all my girlfriends that. You should take it as a compliment."

Shawna forced words through her tightening throat. "I'm not one of your girlfriends either. I'm an actress like you, and I expect to be treated with respect."

"An actress. Really." Penny eyeballed Shawna up and down. "You get a walk-on role and now you're ready to collect your Tony?" Penny's laugh was mocking and shrill.

Judith observed owlishly from the corner, silent yet hanging on every word.

"I didn't say that," Shawna replied, fighting hard to calm the tremor in her voice. "But every company member deserves respect no matter how small the role. Remember, there are no small parts, only small actors."

Penny clapped slowly. "Oh, bravo, bravo. How far did you have to reach up your ass to pull that one out?"

A loud laugh burst from Judith. She clamped a hand over her mouth when Shawna shot her a look.

"All I'm saying--"

"All you're saying is a bunch of bullshit!" Penny had risen out of her chair and was standing before Shawna now, hands on hips. "Your feelings got hurt because of a harmless prank, and you can't let it go."

Shawna knew her face was red, her freckles rising to the surface like bruises on a peach. "It wasn't a prank last night in the basement. You had a real knife."

Penny stepped back, hand to her heart. "You're fucking psycho."

"And you're a slut!" The ugly words exploded from Shawna's mouth like spewing vomit.

The slap which followed was quick and vicious, striking Shawna's left cheek hard.

"Watch who you call names, loser," Penny hissed and brushed past Shawna.

While Shawna stood there, stunned, cradling her stinging cheek, Judith hurried out to fetch Blake, who reacted to the incident with swift professionalism.

Shoving a legal pad under Shawna's nose, Blake instructed her to write down exactly what happened in as much detail as possible. Penny would provide her side of the incident, and Judith would give her, hopefully neutral, eyewitness account. These types of infractions had to be reported to Actor's Equity, Blake explained with a deadpan expression. After all the paperwork was concluded, Shawna and Penny were dismissed from the theater for the day, and an emergency board meeting was called.

Shawna had never felt so ashamed, and once she had pedaled away from the theater, she could no longer hold back the flow of tears. Despite Blake giving her an ice pack, her cheek was tender and swollen. But the shame she felt was far worse than the injury, and now she might lose her job over it. It was all so unfair. Relieved that her Dad hadn't returned from his golf day, Shawna went to her room and collapsed on her bed. She awoke hours later on a damp pillow and her Dad knocking.

"Hey, honey. Dinner's ready."

"I-I didn't know you were home."

"Yeah. Well, I got called to another emergency board meeting at the theater, but luckily I got out of it."

*Thank God!*

"Do you know what that's about?" Bill's voice, muffled behind the door, sounded tired and bored.

"No," Shawna lied.

Shawna rolled over and placed her hand on her cheek. It still ached, but the swelling had subsided. Her Dad might not notice the redness, but she wasn't a good enough actress to conceal her emotions from him.

*I guess I'm not an actress after all.*

"That meatloaf's getting cold."

"I'm not hungry."

"Oh, and why aren't you hungry?"

"Uh, just some hormonal stuff, Dad."

*That'll get rid of him.*

"I'll keep a plate warm for you," he said, retreating down the hall.

Maybe her Dad was right, she thought, staring miserably at the ceiling. Maybe she could get a different internship or a regular old job. She could work at the Tullytown Country Club as a caddy or waitress, just like Penny.

"Ugh." She caught her head in her hands, but she refused to waste another tear. She was fully convinced Penny was in the wrong. Shawna had certainly provoked her by calling her a "slut." Sexual harassment of any kind is formally verboten according to Equity Rules. Shawna recalled, with shame, her Women's Study seminar at Bryn Mawr, which focused on the misogynist language aimed at women's sexuality.

*And yet, the word 'slut' was right there on the tip of my tongue.*

Filled with self-pity and regret, Shawna scrolled through the messages on her phone, wondering why no one had contacted her about the meeting?

Her phone vibrated in her hand, blaring out the Tyler Swift ringtone, *Shake it Off*. God, she wished she could do just that. She fumbled with the phone, dropped it in a panic, but recovered it in time.

"Hello?"

With a rapid heartbeat, Shawna listened as Blake informed her in her usual flat delivery that a decision had been made at the meeting. Penny McNeil was fired and banned from the theater for the season due to her act of physical violence against another actor. Shawna had been found guilty of the lesser infraction of sexual harassment and was given a warning.

A warning was better than termination, but the shame still stung her. She wondered if this was something that would remain on her permanent Equity record, but she was too embarrassed to ask.

"Oh," Blake said as an afterthought, "RJ would like to offer you the role of Cassandra if you want it."

*For real! He's offering me Penny's role?*

Shawna's heart sang. This was--as they say in the business--her big break. But was this the way to get it?

Shawna cleared her throat, and in her most professional voice, she informed Blake that she would love to play Cassandra.

"Fine," Blake responded dryly. "RJ will want to meet with you first thing in the morning. Copy?"

"Yes."

Blake ended the conversation coldly without offering any congratulations. Although the news couldn't have been more favorable for Shawna, the conversation left her feeling empty.

Of course, taciturnity was just Blake's manner. Still, as Shawna dimmed her bedroom light so that the star patterns from the novelty light her Dad had given her on her twelfth birthday shone on the ceiling, she realized with a startling revelation that everything had changed. She was no longer a child, a juvenile. She had risen in the theater ranks in a few short weeks from lowly intern to leading lady.

But had she truly paid her dues?

Shawna spent a long time reflecting on this question while gazing at the slowly revolving constellations casting light and shadows on the bedroom ceiling. And for the first time since the time her Mom died, she tossed and turned for most of the night and barely slept.

# CHAPTER 18

"Well, if it isn't Eve."

Shawna spun around to confront Ron Dee. She had never spoken to him directly. Both Ron and Harriet worked behind the scenes in often overlooked roles: making sure bills were paid, programs printed, and promotional materials mailed to the theater's extensive mailing list.

"Excuse me," Shawna said with forced congeniality. "My name's Shawna."

Shawna thought that the tobacco-stained smile Ron flashed back at her had a wicked edge. His pupils glimmered like dark flames behind his thick eyeglasses.

"Nope," Ron said, gliding past her in his pleated gray trousers, lavender dress shirt, and floral tie. "It's Eve Harrington. Welcome to the big leagues, my dear."

Stunned and confused by Ron's remarks, Shawna continued to the women's dressing room.

*Well, that was weird.*

Judith was already at the ironing board, her eyeglasses fogged from the jetting steam.

"Good morning, Judith."

"Morning? Feels like I never left. There's your new spot." Judith cocked her head at Penny's former makeup table. Shawna gazed at the messy greasepaint sticks and open cold cream jar containing a crushed cigarette butt.

"Don't expect me to clean it up," snapped Judith.

"I don't." Shawna caught her reflection in the lighted mirror and hardly recognized herself. Was it possible that she looked so much older in just a few short weeks? Her eyes, especially, looked world-weary. She recalled wishing she looked older, but now—

She turned her back to the mirror. "Hey, Judith. Who's Eve Harrington?"

Judith fumbled with the iron, almost burnt herself. "Who's Eve Harrington! Don't they teach you anything at your fancy school?"

"Apparently not." Shawna leaned against the makeup table.

"You've never heard of the movie *All About Eve* starring Bette Davis?"

Shawna wasn't fond of old movies, especially black and white ones, but she vaguely knew who Bette Davis was from various Instagram memes: something about Bitches Do It Better.

*Was Ron calling me a bitch?*

Shawna sighed, pondering how annoying Boomers were to Gen-Z.

*Always expecting us to understand their cultural references, yet caring so little for ours.*

"So, Bette Davis play plays Eve Harrington in the movie?" Shawna asked, rubbing her eyes. She was so tired.

Judith sighed with exasperation. "No. Eve Harrington is the little backstabber who worms her way into Margo Channing's life by pretending to be a fan and quote 'nice girl' and ends up stealing Margo's part in the play and her man! A lot like real life, I tell you. Bette Davis plays Margo. I can't believe you never watched it."

Shawna flushed. "Wait. Ron thinks I'm like Eve?"

"Don't mind Ron. He's extra cranky these days because he's lost his drug contacts now that Dougal's toast. But you didn't hear that from me."

Now that Shawna understood the full impact of Ron's insult, she was more angry than hurt.

*Of course, people are going to take their potshots now. Let them!*

Pushing through her fatigue, Shawna cleaned up Penny's mess. When Liz showed up, the dressing room looked neater and smelled fresher.

"Hey, kiddo," Liz said, smiling widely. "Welcome aboard, and good riddance to old rubbish." Liz squeezed herself into the chair before her makeup table and prepared for rehearsal. "I guess you want to run lines." She pinned her black hair, showing an inch of gray roots, away from her face.

"If you don't mind," Shawna said, relieved. "Mr. Jennings, I mean RJ, was supposed to meet me this morning, but I guess he got delayed."

"Delayed, my ass!" Liz said. "Hungover is more like it."

Shawna darted a glance at Judith, who continued to diligently iron, mouth shut and ears open.

"All right," Liz said through a yawn as if she'd gotten little sleep, too. "Let's start with scene one."

∼

Despite Shawna's nervousness about stepping fully into the Cassandra role, the work she'd already done as the understudy had paid off handsomely. The scene with Hutch went exceptionally well. Shawna felt herself swept up in the emotions during their duet. Her singing voice could be better trained, but the music was in her key, and by the end of the number, her confidence soared. Hutch gave her all the support she needed, and for a moment, when Agamemnon cradled the young Cassandra in his arms, Shawna felt the power of the moment.

Except for a few bumpy blocking moments, she only had to call for "line" once, and when the morning rehearsal had concluded, the entire cast applauded her efforts. One glance at RJ told her he was pleased.

Shawna's step was light when she headed back to the dressing room to get her lunch, but when she opened the door, she stopped dead. A stifled scream tore at her throat.

Liz entered behind her. "What happened?"

Reduced to a scared child again, Shawna pointed at the makeup mirror at her station. Scrawled in red lipstick on the glass were the words: YOUR DEAD SLUT!

"Oh, for heaven's sake!" Liz crossed the room and swiped several tissues from the box. "Judith!"

Judith tottered in. "What's up, Mrs. J?"

Liz had already wiped off some of the lipstick from the mirror with tissue. The horrific words--grammatically incorrect but impactful--were erased, but the greasy red smears remained like bloodstains from a crime scene. "Judith, did you see Penny backstage while we were rehearsing? No one else would have done this."

"No," Judith said, energized by the drama. "What did she write?"

"Something disgusting," Liz said. "Get me some Windex, will you?"

While Judith left to find more heavy-duty cleaning supplies, Shawna dropped limply into a chair and stared at the floor.

"Listen, kiddo," said Liz. "That's show biz."

"Really?" Shawna said. "But this is supposed to be a community theater. No offense, but it's not like this is Broadway."

"You're not kidding! When I was an ingenue just starting out..."

Shawna hadn't meant to cue Liz for another long-winded story, but she was too polite to walk away until the older actress was out of wind.

Shawna reported the mirror incident to Blake, but nothing came of it since there were no eyewitnesses. Shawna returned to rehearsal after lunch feeling deflated but determined to keep her chin up.

After running several more challenging numbers in Act Two, everyone but Shawna was dismissed. RJ wanted her to hone her musical numbers with Patricia, the part-time accompanist. Patricia, a quiet older lady with hair styled in a tight gray bun, played organ at the local Presbyterian Church. They would use a pre-recorded orchestral score during the performances because hiring a full orchestra was beyond the theater's budget. While Patricia banged out chords on the baby grand piano Blake had wheeled from the wings onto the stage, Shawna tried hard to push her voice to fill the empty house.

By five o'clock, Shawna was exhausted. She dragged herself back to the dressing room and opened the door cautiously, afraid of finding another threatening note on the mirror, but thankfully the room was untouched.

Fatigued after the long day, Shawna called her Dad, hoping he could give her a ride. His phone rang and rang. She hung up before hearing his voicemail message. She knew her Dad was busy with the case of the missing woman, among his other mayoral obligations. Since finding the abandoned car in the creek, the pesky journalist, Dale Cartwright, had written weekly editorials about the town's lack of leadership--and implied misogyny--regarding the cold case of a woman whom people seemed to have forgotten. All of this reflected badly on Mayor Bill.

Shawna closed the dressing room behind her, but instead of taking the shorter path through the backstage area to reach the parking lot, she decided to walk through the empty house to the front doors and circle back around to where she'd parked her bike. After everything that had happened, Penny's "pranks" and the threatening message on the mirror, she didn't relish the thought of fumbling her way in the dark to the backdoor, even if it was the shortest distance between two points.

Shawna entered the stage from the down right wing. The piano was put away backstage, and only the ghost light kept solitary watch down center, a faint beacon of light in the darkness. Halfway across the stage, Shawna heard thudding footsteps close behind her.

She whirled, expecting to see Blake, who was always the last to leave.

But there was no Blake, only a rustle in the wings.

"Hello?" she called into the backstage darkness.

A quick trill of the piano keys made her jump out of her skin. Someone was backstage and they were messing with her.

Shawna turned and proceeded quickly downstage, but her feet stopped short when she heard a grating noise above her head. She looked up in time to see something flying down from the catwalk.

She jumped out of its way just in time. Losing her footing, she slammed onto the stage, her palms slapping against the boards. Her knee took the rest of the tumble and flamed painfully on impact.

A scream lodged in her throat when she saw a body with a rope around its neck, swinging from the catwalk.

It took Shawna several seconds of heart-stopping fear to realize the body dangling over the stage was the dummy that spooked her in the dressing room. As it swung in a slow arc over the stage, Shawna saw with growing revulsion that the dummy was dressed in a curly red wig and an outfit closely resembling her own style.

More angry than scared, Shawna scrambled to her feet and shouted, "It's not funny, Penny! My Dad will have you arrested!"

Footsteps clattering along the length of the metal catwalk accompanied by maniacal laughter confirmed who it was.

Fighting back tears, Shawna limped down the aisle. Once outside, she called her Dad.

He picked up on the first ring. "I was just about to call you."

"D-Dad?"

"You sound upset. Where are you?"

"Outside the theater," Shawna blubbered.

"I'm just down the street. Be there in a flash."

That night, over dinner at Frank's Pizzeria, Shawna unburdened herself to her Dad, telling him everything about Penny's campaign of torment toward her. His face darkened during the story's latter half, and she wished she'd kept it to herself because she knew what was coming.

He wiped the pizza grease from his chin, wadded up the paper napkin, and tossed it on the empty paper plate. "Listen, honey, I don't think that place is safe for you."

"But, Dad--"

He lifted his hand. "Hear me out. All I ever wanted," he paused to collect himself, "all your Mom and I ever wanted was for you to live out your dreams, to reach for the stars."

Shawna's throat tightened.

"You're all I got now."

Shawna reached out and gripped his hands. Choked with emotion, she could only whisper, "I know."

"And I have to tell you, I have a bad feeling about that place. For one thing," he lowered his voice to ensure no spies were lurking about. He needn't fear. The pizzeria was empty except for a bored-looking teenager mopping the floor. "The people who work there are weird."

"Oh, come on, Dad. They may be a bit eccentric, but--"

"They're weirdos. And a lot of them have problems. Mental health issues, like this Penny. Let's just say she doesn't have the best reputation in town. And don't even get me started on Rick Jennings. He and his wife are notorious drunks."

"Wasn't RJ in recovery? Maybe he just—"

"Recovery, my ass. For all I know, they're doing illegal drugs too."

Shawna shook her head and decided not to mention the rumors she'd heard about Dougal and Ron Dee.

"Remember, honey, I went to school with some of those people. They were weird then, and they're weirder now. And desperate."

"What do you mean desperate?"

Bill shifted his weight on the hard plastic seat. "I shouldn't tell you this, and it's just between us, but the theater is very close to financial ruin. Which is probably why RJ's been spotted at the General Greene every night, drinking away his sorrows, and now that fellow, Dudley Wicks, is threatening to sue, and let me tell you, he has a very strong case." Bill made a face like he smelled something foul. "And what's with this play they're doing? No one wants to see Greek tragedy. If they want to make money, they should go back to doing plays like *Footloose*. That was a sellout."

Shawna leaned forward and cradled her face in her hands. The uneasiness in her gut mixed unfavorably with the two pepperoni slices that she had wolfed down too fast. "It's a musical reinterpretation of a classic play. Dudley Wicks doesn't own the rights to a work that has been in the public domain for over two thousand years."

"Sure, the source material, but what about Wick's original score?"

Shawna shook her head. "It shouldn't matter because the lyrics are translated from the original Greek." She shrugged. "Or, at least, it creates a legal loophole that won't be sorted out until the play is mounted. And then, if it makes a lot of money, RJ can pay off Wicks, save the theater, and everyone will be happy."

"Well, a lot is riding on that *if*."

Shawna straightened and smiled at her Dad. "You know why it's going to make money?"

"Why?"

"Because I'm starring in it, that's why."

Bill shook his head, laughed, and gazed at his daughter with pride. "That's my girl. But with a mind like yours, wouldn't you rather intern at one of the law firms in town?"

Shawna shook her head, determined. "Listen, Dad, if

there's one thing I learned this summer, it's that the show must go on."

Bill stood and rubbed his belly with a groan. "Well, I guess I can't argue with that."

That night, Shawna watched *All About Eve* on TCM. She enjoyed every minute of the film and was surprised that something so outdated could not only be entertaining but also profound. And, having slyly manipulated her Dad to see things from her perspective, she wondered if she wasn't a bit like Eve Harrington after all.

*Maybe*, she thought when she turned out her bedroom light, *I should embrace my inner diva a little bit more.*

## CHAPTER 19

Feeling refreshed and more confident the following day, Shawna entered the theater determined to report the dummy incident, point the finger squarely at Penny, and demand something be done about it. But when she burst through the double doors at the back of the house, the dummy was gone and the theater was empty except for Blake quietly sweeping the stage.

"Hey, Blake," Shawna said, starting down the center aisle. "That dummy that was hanging there--"

"Huh?" Blake looked up and frowned.

Shawna pointed at the catwalk. "The dummy you took down. Penny was the one who did it. I meant to call you last night, but--"

"I don't know what you're talking about," Blake said flatly.

"There wasn't a dummy here when you came in?"

"Nope."

"Were you the first one here?"

"Yup."

Perplexed and feeling a bit like a dummy herself,

Shawna mounted the stage via the side stairs and continued backstage through the stage right wing.

*I know what I saw, and I know it had to be Penny who did it. Or maybe--*

She stopped momentarily and peeked through the curtain at Blake who continued to sweep.

Liz was already in the dressing room when Shawna entered.

"Morning, Liz."

"Howdy, kiddo. I brought some doughnuts." Liz indicated a big pink box on a shelf near the bathroom door.

"Don't tell me you're dieting!" Liz continued when Shawna didn't rush to help herself.

"No. I already ate. I'll take some coffee, though. Thanks, Liz."

Shawna poured herself a cup from the cardboard container and casually leaned against the wall.

"Hey, Liz. How long has Blake been stage manager here?"

Liz put down her coffee cup and shook the doughnut crumbs from her script. "I'm not sure. A few seasons, at least."

"Do you know if she's friends with Penny?"

Liz laughed. "You know they're roommates, right?"

Shawna nearly spit out her coffee. "Roommates? Are you serious?"

"Sure. I thought you knew that."

"Penny and Blake live together? For how long?"

Liz shrugged. "For ages, as far as I know," Liz lowered her voice. "I always suspected Blake had a big crush on Penny. Poor thing. She used to follow her around like a puppy. Then, once Hutch showed up, well. Game over."

"Do you think Blake was hurt?"

"Hey, kiddo. Refill my coffee, will you?" Liz held out her mug.

"Oh, yeah. Sure." Shawna grabbed Liz's mug, noting with some revulsion the lipstick stain on the lip.

"And if there's any chocolate doughnuts left, bring me one. Sure you don't want any?"

"I'm sure."

Shawna dutifully waited on Liz, hoping to draw more information from her. "Do you think Blake's upset that Penny got canned?"

Liz sighed. "I don't know. Stage managers are a different breed from us performers. If you don't mind running these lines for me, Shawna, I sure could use the help." She tapped a finger against her temple. "The old bean's not as sharp as it once was."

∼

DURING THE MORNING REHEARSAL, Shawna struggled to stay focused. RJ had to remind her to speak up twice. She was frustrated by Penny's distracting behavior and suspected that Blake, who was familiar with every corner and secret passage of the theater, was involved. Shawna felt that complaining to RJ would make her seem paranoid. Even Hutch didn't believe her when she recounted what had happened in the basement.

*Maybe Penny and Blake are working together*, Shawna thought during one of the short breaks. *Hutch said Penny was at the bar, so maybe it was Blake in the basement. She was always the last to leave. Of course!*

Shawna shuddered when Blake said, "And we're back" through the God mic, the microphone the stage manager used to make announcements through the PA system.

Shawna returned to rehearsal, determined to keep an eye on Blake from now on. Shawna's Dad had often complained about local politics and the importance of getting the right people on your side. Shawna wondered if she should start using the same tactics.

She quickly surveyed the ensemble, contemplating with whom she should align herself. Liz was maternal toward her, but that was her nature with everyone. As the veteran leading lady, Liz could possibly feel threatened by an up-and-coming talent like Shawna, just as Penny had been with her. RJ was the established figurehead, but his lingering stares at her body sometimes made her uneasy. While she held him in high regard as a mentor, she hesitated to grow too close, worried about sending the wrong impression. That left Rex, who seemed open to her but mostly kept to himself. However, Rex boasted strong Broadway connections, so staying in his good graces was essential.

Shawna scanned the chorus members assembled for their next group number, all Non-Equity actors who couldn't help her advance her career. Then, her eyes settled on Hutch.

Hutch Davis stood at an impressive height with handsome, chiseled features. However, despite his outward appearance, she couldn't help but feel that he was a little older than she liked, and the vanity he had displayed during their brief car ride was a turnoff. Perhaps there was even a touch of naivety in the leading man, but she saw an opportunity. Dumb men could be easily manipulated. Perhaps Hutch could serve as her protector, and if she desired to teach Penny a lesson, he could be much more than that. *Maybe I should—*

Shawna caught herself mid-thought.

*I sound like a scheming bitch. A real Eve Harrington, indeed.*

It was time for Shawna to rehearse her duet with Hutch, the critical scene before Agamemnon enters the palace to confront Clytemnestra. RJ had staged it so that they were far downstage, with Hutch holding Shawna from behind as they both sang out. Shawna had maintained a respectful distance from Hutch during the previous rehearsals, but now she leaned her body into his. Hutch responded by holding her even closer as they expressed words of love and longing.

At the end of the run, Hutch caught up with Shawna in the wings.

"That was amazing," he said. "I was really feeling it that time. You've come a long way in such a short time, Shawna. I admire that."

"Thank you, Hutch." Shawna lowered her chin and gazed up at him through the fringe of her eyelashes. Since discovering Eve Harrington, she'd been watching old movies at night and learning some of the femme fatale tricks. "But it's easy to improve when you have such an incredible co-star."

Hutch's chest visibly puffed from the praise. "I know you've been heading right home after rehearsals, but I'd love to take you to dinner." He lowered his voice and moved in close so that they were almost touching. "Somewhere out of town."

"Excuse me." Blake popped out between two black curtains, unspooling a coil of wires.

Hutch and Shawna jumped back like two teenagers caught necking.

*Oh, well,* thought Shawna. *Now Blake has an excellent story to tell Penny later.*

She looked at Hutch and smiled sweetly as if she were

Scarlett O'Hara flirting with one of her many beaux. "I'd love to."

∽

Shawna called her Dad to tell him she wouldn't be home for supper.

"Everything okay?" he asked.

"Yes. Just having dinner with one of the cast members. I won't be late. Bye."

She hung up before he could ask which cast member. Shawna didn't think her Dad would exactly approve of her going out with a thirty-five-year-old man, even if they were only friends.

As fortune would have it, Bill had given her a ride that morning. Instead of her usual t-shirt and shorts, she wore a yellow and green floral print sundress and cute sandals. Her hair hung down her back in loose curls. Inside the women's dressing room, she applied lipstick and blush and spritzed on some body spray she found in the closet that she suspected was Penny's. The fragrance smelled a bit cheap, reminiscent of strawberry cologne from the drugstore, but perhaps Hutch would appreciate it.

Hutch whistled when he met Shawna in the parking lot. Gallantly opening the passenger door of his Jeep, he helped her climb inside.

Blake, in her usual spot by the back door having a smoke, didn't respond when Shawna waved goodbye.

"I don't think Blake likes me," Shawna said as they drove away from the theater.

Hutch made a face. "What gives you that idea?"

"Didn't you see how she ignored me just now?"

Hutch looked both ways and turned right on the

highway to head out of town. "She's like that with everyone. I wouldn't take it personally."

"Is it true she lives with Penny?"

Hutch's shoulders stiffened, and Shawna wondered if she had spoken too soon.

"As far as I know, they still live together." Hutch gave Shawna a warm smile.

"What? You mean you don't know?"

He sighed. "I guess there's no harm in telling you that Penny and I broke up."

"Oh, I'm sorry." She wasn't expecting this.

"Don't be," he said.

Shawna stopped herself before saying she hoped it wasn't because of her, realizing how vain it sounded.

Hutch sighed and said, "It was a long time coming, and honestly, it's a relief. I care about her, but being a bachelor again is nice." His twinkling eyes made her nervous.

*Wow*, she thought. *This is an actual date. Am I ready for this?*

∼

She definitely wasn't ready for Hutch's pawing and heavy breathing in the car after the meal.

"I like you, Shawna," Hutch said after planting several wet kisses on her cheeks. He then went for her lips, but she turned her head.

"I like you too, but--"

"But?"

"I feel like I'm wrestling an octopus."

Hutch stopped, sank back in his seat, and raked his hand through his hair. "Wow. I'm sorry, Shawna. I guess I got carried away. It's just that you're so beautiful, and to be honest--"

Shawna noted that Hutch often used the phrase *to be honest*, making her wonder if he were anything but.

"I've been thinking about doing this for a long time."

Shawna adjusted the straps of her sundress and flipped down the lighted mirror to check her makeup. Her lipstick had been kissed away, and her entire face looked chapped. She flipped up the mirror with disdain.

"Hutch, I'm not sure we should get involved."

His mouth tightened as he turned on the ignition. They drove out of the restaurant parking lot in silence.

"I hope you understand," she said. Her Olive Garden meal wasn't agreeing with her—such a letdown after her Dad's Italian cooking. She suppressed a burp.

"I understand, all right." Hutch's tone was as flat as some of his line readings.

"What do you understand?" Shawna's discomfort level was elevating by the second.

"That you're a cocktease."

"What!" Shawna practically screamed. "Are you serious?"

Hutch reached across her lap and popped open the glove compartment. She thought he would pull out another one of his playbills and start pontificating about what a great actor he was, but instead, he grabbed a pack of Marlboro Reds and a lighter.

"You smoke?" Shawna said.

He didn't answer her but lowered the window and lit one up. He blew the smoke out the window. "You bitches are all alike."

"Oh, now I'm a cocktease and a bitch. Can you pull over, please, and let me out?" She began digging through her purse to find her phone.

"Go ahead, call Daddy, little girl."

"What the hell is wrong with you?" Her head was spinning from the cheap wine and Hutch's change of demeanor.

"I know you're young, but you're old enough to hear a piece of advice."

"Oh, what's that?"

Hutch was driving fast along the highway now, heading back into town. She wanted to tell him to slow down, but she couldn't get home fast enough.

"You might want to think twice before rubbing your ass against a guy's cock like you did with me during our number today. Someone might think you're asking for it."

Too enraged to speak, Shawna sat with arms crossed, her cheeks burning, until, at last, the lighted sign of her development came into view like a beacon of wholesomeness.

"Right here's fine," she said through gritted teeth.

She couldn't believe it when Hutch squealed to a halt in front of the gate to her development. She unclipped her seatbelt and jumped out of the Jeep. Hutch peeled out before she had a chance to slam the door.

"Fuck you!" she screamed at his blinking red taillights.

One of her neighbors, watering her grass at night, said, "Nice language."

"Fuck you, too," Shawna mumbled, but under her breath. One argument was enough for one night.

When she arrived home, she headed straight for the pool. After cooling down some of her rage, she tried to sneak in the back door wearing just a robe, but Bill confronted her in the kitchen, helping himself to a dish of ice cream.

"What did you do? Go for a swim?"

"Yeah. It's pretty hot out there."

"I'll say. Did you have fun tonight?"

"Yeah. Just went out with a few of the cast members."

"Glad you're making friends," he called after her.

Shawna trudged upstairs, ready to put herself to bed along with any notion of ever again playing the role of femme fatale.

## CHAPTER 20

Tech week, sometimes referred to as "hell week" among theater folk, marked the period in the rehearsal process when all production elements--lights, set, costumes, sound--merged to create artistic unity. All actors must be off-book, have their blocking memorized, and be prepared to perfect their craft leading up to the crucial opening night performance.

Shawna excitedly marked off the days on her desk calendar leading up to the night when she would make her official debut. Knowing her health was important, she resisted the lure of after-rehearsal drinks and late-night gossip sessions to focus completely on her performance. In just three weeks of rehearsal, something extraordinary had happened to Shawna. She had unearthed her true calling, a precious secret she kept to herself.

After years of uncertainty, she had found her life's purpose--acting! By the end of the run, she would earn her Equity card, and the only thing left to do after that would be to plan her move to New York City. She imagined her Dad's face when she told him he'd have to support her for at least a year while she got established. She knew he'd be disappointed with her decision, he would even try to talk her out of it, but when he saw her outstanding performance as Cassandra on opening night, he'd be convinced, along with the rest of the audience, that theater was her destiny. The Greeks were right about the concept of fate.

"You sure got your head in the clouds."

"Oh, I'm sorry, Judith. Did you say something?" Shawna gazed down at Judith, who kneeled before her, adjusting the hem of her long tunic.

"I asked you what you thought of your costume."

"Oh, I love it," Shawna gushed.

It wasn't a lie. Of all the moldy old costumes in stock, Judith had found a decent one for Cassandra. The gossamer white silk, gathered at the shoulders draped elegantly over Shawna's petite frame. At first, Shawna thought the white color would accent her pale skin too much, but RJ insisted on white as a symbol of Cassandra's purity. A red sash and a leather breastplate and belt completed the look.

The breastplate was an impressive piece of leatherwork that bore a tag from the Metropolitan Opera's production of *Aida*. It was one of many pieces a New York costume company had donated to the theater years ago. Shawna was thrilled to be wearing such a piece of theater history. But the breastplate was old, and most of the gold paint had worn away. When she had suggested to Judith the day before that it could be repainted, Judith snapped at her, saying that she intended to do it and that Shawna should "stay in her lane." Shawna was happy to see that, despite Judith's grumpy outburst, the breastplate had been finished with a fresh coat of gold spray paint. It looked great up close and would look even better on stage.

"Judith, do you think I should add some gold bracelets?

Cassandra is a Trojan Princess. Slave or not, I think Agamemnon would want her looking fine."

Judith groaned as she used a chair to hoist herself from the floor. "I was thinking about that. You don't want them rattling during your dance numbers. How about we put the bracelets high on your upper arms like a snake charmer."

Shawna clapped her hands together. "That would be wonderful." She stared at herself in the full-length mirror. The vision of her character was beginning to take shape. "I want to try on my wig to see the entire look."

"It's right there." Judith pointed to a red wig on a Styrofoam head sitting at Shawna's station. It looked like the same wig that Penny had placed on the dummy. Shawna hesitated before it, wondering if it had some bad "theater vibes" or something.

"What?" barked Judith. "Don't you like it?"

"I love how you styled it, and the gold headband is a nice touch."

Judith beamed from the praise. "You'll need a wig cap. I put some in the drawer at your station."

"Oh, okay." Shawna opened her drawer and screamed.

"What's wrong?" asked Judith, scampering close to Shawna to take a look. "Is there a cockroach in there or something?"

"Not a cockroach, but look what someone did to my headshot?" Shawna picked up the scattered remains of her black and white headshot and let the pieces sift through her fingers. The photo had been taken a few days ago to be displayed in the lobby with the rest of the casts'. It was Shawna's first headshot and she was proud of it.

Judith's hot breath fanned her cheek. "How do you like that?"

Shawna slammed the drawer and wheeled on Judith,

looking her straight in the eye. "Do you have any idea who did this?"

Judith calmly shook her head. "None whatsoever. Nothing like this ever happened at this theater until you came along."

Shawna couldn't help her voice from rising. "Are you implying I'm to blame for this?"

Judith stepped back and shrugged. "I'm just saying it's never happened before. But what do I know?" Deep sigh. "I'm just the wardrobe lady." Judith calmly attended to Liz's elaborate wig, adjusting the pin curls in front.

Panting mad, Shawna whipped off the costume, nearly tearing out a row of stitches, and flung it on the back of her makeup chair. She grabbed the blue kimono robe she had found in stock and tied it around her as she exited the dressing room. She walked through the wings and surveyed the stage. The actors were still on break, and the carpenter over-hires were hard at work constructing the set, consisting of an upstage panorama and a raked platform supporting four large Doric columns. Shawna discovered Blake adjusting a light on a very tall ladder.

"Blake," she called up from the stage. "I need to talk to you about something important."

Blake continued to rotate the light. "Yeah, what's that?"

"I'd appreciate it if you would come down here. It's hard to explain."

"Write it down and put it in the mail then," came the terse reply.

"Excuse me?" Shawna's voice squeaked. She realized she sounded girlish, perhaps even a bit bratty, but didn't care. She was being harassed, and she wouldn't stand for it.

Blake finally stopped what she was doing and glared down at her. "What's the problem?"

"Someone cut my headshot into tiny pieces and put it in the drawer of my makeup table." As soon as the words flew from her mouth, she felt foolish.

Blake laughed. "So, that's your big emergency?"

"Listen. I'm tired of this crap. Penny's been harassing me, and it's going to stop now!" Shawna couldn't believe it when she actually stomped her foot.

"Is our new leading lady having a temper tantrum already?"

Shawna whirled to see Ron leaning against the proscenium wall, watching her with amusement.

"Apparently so." Blake pulled a wrench from her tool belt and tightened the swivel adjustment on the light.

Ron tipped an imaginary hat to Shawna with a sarcastic smile and walked down the side stairs whistling *How Lovely to be a Woman*.

Shawna's face was on fire. "Well, if the stage manager," she called up to Blake, "won't take this seriously, I'll have no choice but to go to RJ."

She heard Blake reply, "You do that."

Shawna stomped off into the darkened wing and immediately collided with the new Genie lift, banging her knee. The pain triggered a flood of tears, and by the time she located RJ in the lobby, she was sobbing. Luckily, he was alone. On his knees, he dug through the small refrigerator behind the concessions counter where the soft drinks were kept.

"I know I hid a beer in here somewhere," he mumbled through gritted teeth.

"RJ, I need to talk to you." Shawna leaned on the concession stand counter and pulled a paper napkin from the holder to blot her eyes and blow her nose.

"Eureka!" RJ smiled as he emerged from the refrigerator,

triumphantly holding aloft a frosted can of Michelob. "Ah, Shawna, what seems to be the problem?" RJ's eyes dropped to Shawna's bare legs in her short robe and lingered there.

"Someone is harassing me, leaving weird messages in my dressing room. Then, a dummy dropped down from the catwalk last night when I was crossing the stage. It scared the crap out of me, not to mention it almost hit me. And now my headshot has been torn into tiny pieces. I'm telling you, Penny is tormenting me because I took her role." Her words sounded ridiculous in her ears. She wondered if RJ would now think she was some neurotic, or worse, paranoid loose cannon the theater couldn't afford to keep around. Perhaps he'd fire her on the spot.

RJ took a long sip of his beer and smacked his lips. His eyes rolled back with pleasure.

Shawna wondered if he'd even heard a word she said and was about to leave in frustration when RJ emerged from behind the concession stand and draped his arm around her shoulders.

"You know, my dear," he said. "You gotta be tough in this business. If someone hates you, take it as a compliment." He squeezed her shoulders tightly. "It means they consider you a threat, and if they consider you a threat, it means you got it." He gave her one last squeeze before heading toward the double doors, enjoying the last of his beer.

Shawna sighed, the wind knocked out of her sails.

*Perhaps RJ is right about me needing to toughen up.*

Holding her head high, she left the lobby and traveled quickly down the center aisle, feeling self-conscious in her short robe. RJ was already settled in his spot front and center, readying himself for the next run-through. Blake was seated at the tech table, a temporary platform set up in the center of the house. A graduate student from Temple

University had been hired to run lights. The bearded young man beside Blake fiddled with the levers on the light board, brought the spots up and down, and made the stage colors dance.

Blake announced into the God-mic. "Welcome back, cast. Please get into costume and get ready to run Act Two."

Shawna rushed across the stage to change. As the lights dimmed, someone grabbed her from behind.

"I saw you cozying up to RJ. I guess he holds more power than me."

The lights came up red on Hutch's angry face.

"Please!"

Shawna wriggled out of Hutch's grasp and returned to the dressing room, wishing she had kept quiet about Penny's harassment. Now, it seemed that everyone had turned against her. Judith stood behind Liz, helping her with her wig. Their voices quieted when Shawna entered.

She quickly got into her costume. Judith stepped up behind her to help with the wig.

"I can manage myself," Shawna snapped.

Judith made a dramatic show of lifting her hands in the air. "Well, ex-CUSE me!"

Shawna saw Judith and Liz exchange a look in the mirror.

*Fuck them!* Shawna thought, tucking the loose strands of her hair beneath the wig cap.

*They think I'm a diva now? Well, I'll show them a diva!*

## CHAPTER 21

Shawna entered the spotlight and began her solo number. Too humble to ever call herself a singer, she had nevertheless been part of the high school choir and had even competed and placed in the county chorus competition. She wished she had continued with her singing in college, but now she was making up for lost time. Her alto range was limited, but she had an excellent ear, and she had learned during the weeks leading up to the final dress rehearsal how to project her voice and make it connect to the emotions conveyed in the lyrics.

Shawna understood Cassandra's struggle as a young woman who tried to speak out, yet no one believed her. Hadn't Shawna tried to tell Hutch and Blake about what Penny was doing? Even RJ had brushed off her concerns.

By the end of Cassandra's sorrowful dirge, real tears fell from Shawna's eyes. The lights changed from melancholy lavender shades to a fiery red as Cassandra squared her shoulders and turned to make her slow walk upstage to the palace doors to face her fate with a resigned dignity. At the blackout, RJ clapped and whistled.

"Phew, I did it," Shawna mumbled to herself as she navigated the tricky turntable set piece behind the palace doors and found her way to the women's dressing room in the semi-darkness.

Blake's voice rasped through the staticky God-mic, "Okay folks, we're not taking a full intermission because of time. So, please take a quick break and prepare to run Act Two."

Judith was waiting for Shawna to help with her costume change.

"Did you hear that Dudley Wicks is still in town?" Asked Judith.

"Really?" She was curious about Wicks' whereabouts, especially after spotting him driving through town.

Judith continued excitedly, "He and Rex were having dinner at Angelo's last night, but you didn't hear that from me."

Shawna had been to Angelo's a few times with her Dad. It was considered Tullytown's finest restaurant, even though "foodie" Mayor Bill secretly declared it overpriced and basic.

"I didn't realize Wicks and Rex were such close friends," Shawna said, changing into Iphigenia's costume.

Shawna recalled how she had overheard Rex's phone conversation. It must have been Wicks on the other end. And now Wicks was in town, just in time for the final dress rehearsal slated for tomorrow night. She wondered if he dared show his face and what would happen if he did.

"Friends!" Judith blurted out with a loud laugh. "They are more than friends." She lowered her voice. "If you ask me, Rex is the one to watch out for."

"What makes you say that?" Shawna picked up a makeup brush to apply fresh powder over the bright blush on her cheeks. Iphigenia needed to have an innocent look.

"Rex acts like everyone's friend, but turn your back, and you'll find a knife in it, metaphorically speaking."

Recalling a line from her freshman British literature class, Shawna said, "Look the innocent flower, but be the serpent under it."

"What's that supposed to mean?" Judith asked as she removed the Iphigenia wig from the stand.

Shawna rolled her eyes. She didn't expect Judith to catch the Shakespearean reference. "It's a quote from Macbeth."

A shrill scream rattled every nerve in Shawna's body; she was surprised the mirrors didn't crack from the sound. She twisted in her seat to see Liz standing on the threshold, looking every inch the tragic heroine in her festooned black wig and gold pleated cape over a gauzy tunic.

"What is it?" Shawna said, alarmed.

"No, you didn't," whispered Judith, who had dropped limply into a chair, looking as if she were about to faint.

Liz's face was frozen in the same bizarre look, eyes bugged open like some silent movie star.

Shawna banged a hairbrush on the table in frustration. "Will someone please tell me what the hell's going on?"

"Y-you said it," Liz thundered. "You said the name of the Scottish play."

Shawna laughed at the ridiculousness. "You mean Macbeth?"

Judith and Liz both screamed in unison.

Liz charged at Shawna, grabbing her by the shoulders and hefting her from the chair. Dragging Shawna to the door, Liz screamed, "Out! Get out! You've cursed us!"

Judith moaned and covered her face with her hands.

Shawna yanked herself from Liz's grip when they reached the door. "Are you psycho? Let go of me!"

Blake rushed in as the two women were struggling. "Break it up!" She cried, squeezing in between them.

Liz leaned against the wall and clutched her chest as if a heart attack was on deck. She took a moment to collect her breath. Lifting a trembling finger, she pointed at Shawna. "This, juvenile." She spat the word as if it were poison. "Said the name of the Scottish play in the dressing room!"

"Uh oh," said Blake. She shook her head and glanced at the ceiling.

"I still don't understand," said Shawna.

"Twenty-five years in this theater," Liz's voice thundered with outrage, "and never once has anyone been so stupid, so fucking amateur!"

After delivering her final verdict, Liz turned with fluttering skirts and sailed out the door. Judith fumbled into her apron pocket, pulled out an inhaler, and began huffing on it.

Shawna burst into tears, destroying her carefully applied eye makeup. "I still don't understand what I did wrong," she wailed.

Blake stood over her, hands on hips. "You broke one of the cardinal rules in the theater. You never, EVER say that name in a theater, especially backstage."

"Why?" asked Shawna, swiping several tissues from the box to daub under her eyes.

"Something about a curse. I don't have time to explain. Intermission is almost over." Blake waved her finger at Shawna. "Com'ere."

Shawna gazed up suspiciously. She trusted none of these theater people. Her Dad was right. They're all nuts!

"I said, com'ere," Blake insisted with a condescending wave. "Go outside the dressing room."

Shawna reluctantly obeyed. She thought this was ridiculous, a silly superstition. She stood outside the door, arms crossed. "Okay. Now what?"

By now, the entire cast had gathered outside the dressing room. Everyone had changed into their Act Two costumes, and they watched with a mix of contempt and amusement as Shawna spun around three times, spat over her left shoulder, and cursed according to Blake's instructions.

Shawna chose the curse word "shit" because that was exactly how she felt. Hutch looked at her as if she were the lowest creature on the planet, and everyone avoided her after the Act Two run.

When it was finally time to go home, Shawna sat forlornly at the dressing room table, wiping off her makeup with tissues and cold cream. Liz wandered in to change, followed by Judith. Both women were stony-faced and silent.

Shawna tossed the used tissue into the trashcan and sighed. "Liz, I'm sorry about what happened."

Liz removed her wig and cap and undid the pins in her hair. "Well, I just hope the production isn't cursed now." Her mouth was tight.

"You don't believe that's true, do you?"

RJ came bounding in, all smiles, before Liz could answer. "How are you ladies doing?" He rested his hands on Liz's shoulders.

Shawna decided it was best to be upfront about it. "Well, everyone is upset with me because I said the name of the Scottish play."

RJ shrugged. "Oh, you mean Macbeth?"

Shawna leaped to her feet and pointed at RJ. "You-you just said it!"

RJ rested his head on his wife's shoulder as they both fell out laughing.

## Final Dress

"Wait!" cried Shawna. "What did I miss?"

Still shaking with laughter, RJ raised his head and said, "You're allowed to say it only if you've played the role, and I have, once at Circle in the Square, once at Shakespeare in the Park..."

Judith leaned in close behind Shawna to retrieve the laundry basket and whispered in her ear, "Duh. Everybody knows that."

~

SHAWNA'S ENERGY had dropped so much from the stress of the dress rehearsal, coupled with her humiliation over the *Scottish Play* incident, that her legs could barely pump the pedals of her bike. She hated herself for not knowing a common theater superstition but hated the cast more for making fun of her, especially Liz.

At dinner, her Dad noticed her sour mood as they sat down to eat. "What's wrong? Is the glitter starting to wear off?"

Shawna wouldn't give her Dad the satisfaction of proving him right about her Thespian adventure. "No, I'm just tired from the performance. Tomorrow night is the final dress rehearsal. We can invite people to watch if you'd like to come."

Bill tossed the green salad with a chef's flair using long wooden tongs. "It depends. What time?"

"We have a musical run in the morning without costumes, then take our meal break at five, and the final dress starts at seven."

"I'll try." He sat down and pushed a plate of steaming meatloaf toward his daughter. "You better eat up. You'll need your strength."

He needn't ask her twice. Her Dad made the best meatloaf, and she dug in with gusto. After she had eaten a large helping, she began working on the mashed potatoes, made extra yummy with Bill's homemade gravy.

"Make sure you eat some of this salad too," he said.

"I will. Hey, Dad?"

"Yeah?" He took an ample bite of his own creation and hummed with approval.

"Do you know that there is a superstition about saying 'Macbeth' in a theater?"

Bill shrugged. "Of course. Everyone knows that."

Shawna slammed down her napkin. "How come I'm the only one who didn't know that?"

Bill buttered a piece of bread and gave her a wry look. "Why? Did you curse your production or something?"

"Oh, no," she lied, filling her salad bowl. "Someone mentioned it. That's all."

Before she went to sleep that night, Shawna opened her laptop and boned up on the *Scottish Play* curse. Legend had it that a coven of real witches had placed the curse on the production in Shakespeare's time because they were unhappy with the Bard's unflattering portrayal of them. She read with keen interest how productions as far-ranging as Laurence Olivier at London's Old Vic to comedian Chris Rock being slapped at the Oscars were due to someone's careless uttering backstage.

She didn't believe in witches or curses, and the only weird sisters she knew were the likes of Liz and Judith. And Penny, of course, must be part of a coven of one. Shawna stretched her arms overhead and yawned.

*I don't need to be friends with any of those clowns. All I need to do is get through this final dress rehearsal and then kill it on opening night.*

A message from an account she didn't recognize appeared on her Facebook app.

She sat bolt upright, her spine tingling when she read the message: **Tis the eye of childhood, That fears a painted devil.**

Shawna recognized the Lady Macbeth quote. Someone from the theater was taunting her.

*It's Penny! It has to be.* Shawna thought, furiously clicking on the page that had only been created that day. The profile name was Lady M.

*Very funny.*

The profile picture showed a tragedy mask, similar to the one Penny had worn when she chased Shawna the first time.

Shawna hovered her fingers over the mouse pad, considering an appropriate comeback. But how should she respond? Would a response make the harassment worse?

Too tired to think straight, Shawna blocked the account, clicked out of the page, and closed her laptop. Tonight, of all nights, she needed rest. Tomorrow was the final dress rehearsal, her last chance to perfect her performance before it would be presented to the world--or at least to the Tullytown theater opening night audience. But she knew there would be reviewers in that audience as well. A *Philadelphia Inquirer* performing arts reporter would probably be there, and New York agents often sent their reps, especially if the play had generated some pre-opening buzz as Wicks' productions usually did. If Shawna gave an excellent performance, as she fully intended to, it could be her ticket to securing a New York agent.

*But don't get ahead of yourself.*

She relaxed into the softness of her pillows and closed her eyes. She had let small-town folks with even smaller minds get the better of her. None of this harassment would have happened if she had stayed in her lane and played the mousy little intern content with sewing on buttons and fetching water for the cast. But she had proven herself to be more than that. If people hated her for that, so be it.

She turned in the bed and hugged one of the pillows against her chest. The moon was high and bright, waxing gibbous, right on the brink of reaching its full potential.

*The moon's trajectory can't be stopped, and neither can mine.*

But even as she closed her eyes, the haunting words "Macbeth does murder sleep" played on a loop inside her mind, making a night's rest nearly impossible.

## CHAPTER 22

The final rehearsal day was divided into two parts: a *sitzprobe*, during which the cast gathered in a circle and sang all the songs to the orchestra track while the crew put the finishing touches on the set and then the final dress rehearsal after the evening meal break.

The theater's reputation among crewmembers, recruited from Philly and New York, had suffered since Dougal's demise. Finding adequate workers was tough, and when half the crew failed to show up that morning, the bulk of responsibilities fell on Blake's shoulders.

One piece of complicated stage business was a consistent problem: the revolving stage, designed to seamlessly shift the setting from the palace's exterior to the interior, never worked correctly. Dougal had constructed a sturdy enough deck with caster wheels attached around a central bearing. Still, despite the new wiring, the motor running it tended to overheat and blow multiple circuits. RJ considered cutting it completely, but Blake insisted she could make it work.

Now, gathered in the lobby with the entire cast, Shawna

felt a palpable energy of camaraderie in the room as everyone worked through their songs, excited about what was to come.

Liz seemed to have forgotten Shawna's faux pas in the dressing room the previous night. *The show must go on!* Was the motto, and everyone seemed to be feeling it. Even Hutch appeared to have gotten over his bruised ego when he gave Shawna a thumbs-up at the end of her number.

RJ gave a little speech before they broke for their meal break.

"I'm so proud of this cast," he said, standing before the group. "This has been a difficult season so far, marked by trouble and tragedy."

Shawna looked around at the cast, who hung on to their director's every word. Some were even tearing up. She noticed, however, that Rex was nowhere to be seen. Was it because his part was done, or was there some other reason?

"But," RJ continued. "We all pushed through the challenges, and tomorrow night, when this play opens, we will present something so unique and so brilliant that I have no doubt it will be a night to remember, a true night in the theater." He raised his hands. "So, bravo to all of you and Godspeed!"

Applause followed by jovial chatter filled the lobby as the cast congratulated each other. Shawna found herself caught up in the excitement as well. Past mistakes and disagreements were forgotten. All that mattered now was the show and everyone coming together to make it happen.

Shawna's elation, however, quickly faded when she caught sight of Ron standing in the office doorway, his gaze conspicuously fixed on her. Through the window of Ron's office, she could see Harriet staring at the cast through the window, but especially at her. Ron's lips formed a crocodile smile as if he could read Shawna's thoughts.

*Ignore him,* she told herself. *He's just bitter, old--*

The lobby door crashed open, and Penny staggered in wearing denim shorts and a rumpled T-shirt. Her hair was a chaotic mess, her makeup smeared. She appeared drunk when she made an unsteady path toward RJ.

Everyone froze except RJ, who addressed his former star player with fatherly patience. "Penny, my dear, you know you're not supposed to be here. Those are Equity rules, not mine."

But when RJ attempted to gently guide Penny toward the door, she wiggled from his grip and almost toppled over her platform sandals.

"Equity Smeckity," Penny slurred. "I wonder what Actor's Equity would say about a director." She pointed at RJ. "Fucking one of his actresses while she was still in high school?"

RJ's suave composure vanished in an instant. He tried to grab Penny's arm, but she slipped from his grip. She scanned the cast's stunned faces, landing on Shawna's. "I guess you know all about it, don't you?"

Shawna no longer felt any fear of Penny, only pity. She was pathetic, and now she had made a complete ass of herself in front of everyone. Shawna's silent contempt seemed to provoke Penny to sink to lower depths.

Penny moved so close to Shawna's face that she could smell the vodka on her breath. "Does Liz know you're fucking her husband and probably everyone else in the cast?"

Liz, who had silently snuck up behind Penny, shouted, "That's enough!" in a theatrically booming voice that echoed off the lobby ceiling. Penny turned, her mouth agape and ready to spill more venom, when Liz slapped her hard on the cheek. Rattled, Penny stood shocked for moment then sank to the floor in ugly sobs.

"Will somebody get her out of here? For Heaven's sake, where's Blake?" RJ shouted.

Blake raced across the room, yanked Penny off the floor, and rushed her out the door. Hutch dropped into a chair, head in hands. The good energy from the morning's rehearsal was swept away in a moment's chaos. Shawna noticed Ron standing in the office doorway with a smug look as if entertained by the spectacle. Harriet looked up from her desk with a rictus grin plastered on her face, making Shawna shudder.

*What's up with these two? It's almost as if they knew Penny would make an appearance and were anxiously waiting for it to happen.*

Shawna couldn't wait to give her best performance and move on from this den of weirdos. Professional theater in New York had to be better than this insane asylum.

∽

THE CAST GATHERED at the General Green Inn during their dinner break. Shawna, who had worked up an enormous appetite, sat alone in the corner booth devouring a Philly cheesesteak. It was perhaps too heavy of a meal before a big performance, but she needed the energy. She skipped the onions out of respect for her fellow cast mates. But just in case, she kept a supply of breath mints in her makeup kit, along with honey and lemon throat lozenges, and she also stored a thermos of hot tea at her station. She was learning the tricks of the trade.

The Penny incident had upset everyone. RJ stood at the

bar, slinging back his third neat Irish whiskey. Liz was beside him, a motherly arm draped around his neck. Whatever the truth of Penny's big reveal, the incident seemed to have brought the couple closer together.

*George and Martha can't be parted no matter what*, Shawna thought, returning her attention to her cheesesteak.

Shawna was about to take another bite when Hutch caught her eye and gestured if he could join her. She quickly wiped her mouth with the paper napkin and nodded yes.

Hutch sheepishly approached, holding a draft beer. He slid into the booth across from her.

"How are you doing, Shawna? Are you ready for tonight?"

"Yes," she said. "I can't wait. I just hope that turntable works."

"Me too. Hey, I'm really sorry about Penny."

Shawna shrugged. "It's not your fault. You can't help it if your ex-girlfriend is psycho."

Hutch made a half-hearted laugh. "She's sensitive like a lot of actors. But I probably made the situation worse by involving you."

"Involving me?" Shawna wanted to forget their "date" had ever happened, and she hoped he'd forget it too.

"I told her about us," Hutch confessed with a naughty little boy smirk.

Shawna shook her head. "Hutch, there is no us."

He cocked an eyebrow at her. "Really?"

"Yes, really. I think you're a great guy, but I'm not ready to date anyone now."

He nodded. "I understand. Maybe by the end of the run you'll change your mind."

She took a long sip on her Coke to avoid saying she wouldn't. What would her Women's Studies seminar have to say about the female instinct to protect a man's ego? Why not just give him a firm *no*, and if he doesn't accept that an even firmer *fuck off!*

Hutch took a swig of beer, wiped his mouth, and said with a smile, "That Penny can be wild sometimes." The twinkle in Hutch's eyes made Shawna wonder if he didn't find Penny's erratic behavior exciting on some level.

"Just keep her far away from me," Shawna said, sorry she had allowed Hutch to join her. Her appetite spoiled, she put down her sandwich.

Hutch eyed his reflection in the window by the booth and said, "Maybe I'm prejudiced, but I don't think Penny would act as crazy--I mean, act the way she does, if it weren't for men like RJ taking advantage of her."

Hutch had a point. "Did that really happen when she was in high school?" Shawna inquired in a lowered voice.

Hutch shifted his gaze to her. "It's possible. Many powerful men in this town took advantage of Penny, if you know what I mean." His eyes narrowed.

Shawna despised guessing games. In her best snobby Brynn Mawr accent that would have made Hepburn proud, she asked, "To whom exactly are you referring? That old doctor whose wife killed herself?"

Hutch settled back in the booth. The smile and dimples vanished, and his eyes glimmered with the hardness of cut gems. "Yeah, that doctor was one, but there were many others." He slid out of the booth, stood, drained his beer, and slapped the empty glass on the table. "You should look into your father's involvement with Penny and, while you're at it, Candace Laherty."

Stunned, Shawna gaped at him. Rising in her seat she said, "Are you seriously suggesting my father had an affair with Penny and this--this missing woman?" She realized her voice had projected loudly through the tavern, so much so that everyone was now staring at her.

Hutch smirked at her and said, "See you on stage, Shawna."

The cast and crew returned to their drinks and their gossip. Fully in his cups now, RJ appeared oblivious to the entire exchange.

Shawna signaled Eddie for the check. So much for the temporary camaraderie among the cast, Shawna thought as she pulled cash from her jeans pocket and placed it on the bill. She had gotten a ride to the inn with RJ and Liz, but the thought of driving even a short distance with drunks was out of the question.

She wriggled out of the booth and made her escape through the side door. Standing alone in the parking lot, gazing beyond the traffic light at the rolling highway, she wondered what she should do now. The theater was less than a mile away, but she didn't relish walking along the side of the highway. She pulled out her phone and called her Dad.

"What a coincidence," Bill said, the wind of his open car window distorting his voice. "I'm heading toward the theater right now. My meeting was canceled tonight, so I can attend your final dress rehearsal, after all."

"Wonderful," said Shawna, relieved, her heart bursting with love for her Dad. He was always there for her in a pinch, always willing to set things right.

## CHAPTER 23

During the quick ride to the theater, Bill was full of questions: "How was Shawna feeling? Was she nervous? Excited? Was she glad her ole Dad was there to cheer her on?"

Shawna answered truthfully that she was more excited than nervous and absolutely thrilled he was there, but she also craved some time alone to collect herself.

Bill parked near the willow tree and gave his daughter a curious look. "Are you sure you're okay, hon? You seem tense."

"I'm just focused, Dad," Shawna replied, a bit too sharply.

It was her last chance to perfect her performance, to receive final notes from RJ, and for the crew to (hopefully) work out the remaining technical kinks. She shoved what Hutch had told her to the farthest reaches of her mind. Hutch was as unstable as Penny, Shawna decided. Just in a different way. She'd never trust him again, that's for sure. But despite her personal feelings toward her co-star, she had to put that all aside for tonight's rehearsal.

"I've got to get ready, Dad," Shawna said, planting a quick peck on Bill's cheek.

Bill checked his watch. "When does this thing start?"

"This *thing* starts at eight." She swung open the passenger door.

"So, I have a half hour to kill." He left the car running, the AC blasting.

"Dad, I can't be late." Shawna hopped out and jogged toward the backdoor.

"Don't worry about me," Bill called after her. "I've got some calls to make and..."

She didn't catch everything he said because she had to sign in at half-hour according to Equity rules. The last thing Shawna needed for her career path was another infraction preventing her from getting her Equity card.

In a few months' time, if everything went as planned, she'd be moving out of her childhood home and into her first New York apartment. She imagined a studio on a cobblestone street in the West Village. She hadn't told her Dad about her plans yet, which would come later after her opening night triumph.

*One step at a time.*

After signing the call sheet, she stared at her name. Shawna Anthony sounded so plain, a dime-a-dozen name.

*Perhaps I'll change it to something more exciting and memorable.*

Antonia Shaw had a nice ring to it.

*I'll think about it.*

Shawna moved to the dressing room with a light step. Liz was already seated before her lighted make-up mirror, applying liquid eyeliner, which Shawna thought looked a bit too Egyptian, but she dared not say anything.

"Good evening," Shawna said.

Liz smiled in the mirror. "There you are. I was wondering if you might have cold feet or something." Liz carefully lifted an eyelash with tweezers and placed it on her eyelid.

"Seriously?" Shawna couldn't help but make a face. "Why would I do that?" Shawna sat at her station, feeling slightly annoyed.

Liz blinked in the mirror. "Stranger things have been known to happen in this place. Listen, kiddo..."

Liz spun in her chair to face Shawna, who braced herself for another uncomfortable exchange.

"Maybe I've been a little tough on you," Liz said.

Shawna was about to insist it wasn't a problem, even though it was, but Liz stopped her with an upheld hand.

"I'm not sure how you rose in the ranks so fast. But the fact is, you have, and I suppose I should admire you for that. But let me tell you something." Liz pointed a finger at Shawna as she had with the Macbeth gaffe, but more good-naturedly this time. Shawna wondered caustically if it was Liz's signature stage gesture and that perhaps she should develop a new one. "If I were twenty years younger and thirty pounds lighter, I'd give you a run for your money."

*Try eighty pounds lighter, but whatever you say.*

Recalling her Dad's advice about the importance of diplomacy, Shawna forced a sweet smile and said, "Liz, I hope you and I can become good friends during the run. I wish you the best, really. And good luck tonight!"

Liz threw up her hands. "Don't say good luck! It's break a leg! Haven't you learned anything? At least you didn't say it on opening night. That would be unforgivable."

Shawna shook her head, laughed, and shouted, "I can't win!"

*Final Dress* 173

∽

THEATER FAUX PAS BE DAMNED, Shawna now stood fully costumed, wigged, and made-up, waiting in the wings for her first entrance. Liz neared the end of her first solo number, a dramatic ballad about her rage at Agamemnon's arrogance and how she had taken a new lover, Aegisthus, whom RJ had written out of the script. But nonetheless, he was a presence offstage.

Shawna pressed her eye to the seam between the downstage side flat and the proscenium curtain. Perhaps it was an amateur move to peek at the audience, but she was curious. She spotted her Dad in the second row thumbing through an advanced copy of the program.

*Ugh. Is he bored already?*

Knowing her Dad, he was probably just checking to ensure the Mayor's Office was sufficiently thanked somewhere on the program's pages.

Scanning the empty rows, she spotted RJ seated all the way in the back of the house, slumped down with his fingers steepled below his beard. His expression was hard to read. Was he pleased as his speech earlier in the day had expressed, or did he secretly believe it was a disaster, a turkey that wouldn't fly, and that's why he'd started drinking again?

Seated a few rows from the back of the house, was Rex, exuding an air of nonchalance. Shawna wondered if he was counting the minutes before he could head back to New York. She recalled his phone conversation in the lobby. If Rex had been speaking with Wicks, there didn't seem to any sign of him. Not yet anyway.

"Ready, Shawna?"

She turned to gaze at Hutch, tall and handsome in a short red chiton, gold breastplate and helmet, and lace-up sandals. Shawna thought he looked like a cross between Alexander the Great and a Chippendale dancer.

"I'm ready," she said, suppressing a burp. The cheesesteak had been a mistake.

As the recorded orchestra's triumphant music swelled, signaling the end of Clytemnestra's number, Hutch and Shawna prepared for their entrance.

"Milady?" Hutch held out his hand and gallantly helped Shawna onto the chariot. Despite their minimal rehearsal time with the stage chariot, Shawna couldn't help but wonder if walking onto the stage would have been a more logical choice. The horse harnessed to the chariot, rented from a prop house, looked far from realistic. The plan to hire a live horse and handler from a local farm had fallen through. Shawna found the choice silly and embarrassing even, but RJ was determined to stick to his vision.

"Break a leg, Cassandra," whispered Hutch, lifting the reins attached to the fake horse's harness. Gone were the sour words between them. They were back to playing their roles, which suited Shawna just fine.

"Break a leg," Shawna replied.

As the spotlight on Clytemnestra gradually dimmed, a subtle round of applause filled the theater. The lights brightened, and the chariot was yanked forward onto the stage via a pulley rope.

The fake horse and the chariot's less-than-smooth entrance drew a giggle from her Dad. She told herself to focus. RJ had reminded the cast that the play didn't come alive until it was performed in front of an audience, that there was no theater without an audience, even if it was only an audience of one.

Hutch alighted from the chariot and performed his scene with Liz while Shawna waited, head bowed inside the chariot. Again, Shawna questioned RJ's blocking choice. Couldn't she, as Cassandra, just pick up the reins and gallop away from the palace? Shawna stole a quick glance at the plastic animal and thought, *fat chance*. The spotlight baked the top of her head. Not all of the Fresnels had been replaced by LEDs. Sweat gathered around the edge of her wig. The urge to scratch her scalp became overpowering. Hutch and Liz performed their duet, a song where Clytemnestra pretends to be the loving wife welcoming her husband home after a long battle, but Cassandra knows what fate awaits them.

With a sweep of her silver-embroidered robe, Liz exited the stage. Mayor Bill politely applauded.

*At least Dad didn't leave,* Shawna thought, stealing a quick glance in his direction. Her gaze flicked to the back of the house and she noticed that both RJ and Rex were gone. She had hoped to have their full attention during her number. It would be her last chance to make any necessary changes to her performance. More than anything, Shawna wanted to be perfect for opening night.

Hutch made a slow arc downstage and held out his hand for Shawna. The chorus of Argive elders entered and began their doleful dirge. The lighting changed as Hutch and Shawna moved downstage to perform their duet. To avoid any distracting eye contact with her Dad, Shawna fixed her eyes on the back wall while she sang. She noticed shadows moving inside the booth. RJ and Rex must have gone up there to check on a light cue or something. She reminded herself to focus.

Hutch's voice sounded strong, and their harmony blended well. The stupid horse and chariot unit was supposed to glide effortlessly into the wings during their number, but instead, it got caught on a masking side curtain. Shawna could barely hang on to her concentration till the end of the song.

Her Dad applauded loudly when it was over.

Hutch's Agamemnon spoke a few lines downstage before he made a dramatic sweep with his billowy red silk cape and walked upstage and through the palace doors to meet his fate.

Shawna held her position downstage while the lights changed. She heard muttered curses behind her as one of the stagehands untangled the horse and chariot from the curtain and shoved it into the wings. A clanging on the catwalk above her provided further distraction, but she didn't dare look up and ruin the scene. Perhaps a light had burnt out, and one of the few crew members who'd bother to show up was fiddling around with it.

It was her cue. She raised her head and made a slow promenade around the stage until she found her mark, a small X of black gaffer's tape on the floor. A light bathed her in melancholy blue as she began singing woefully of impending death and her helplessness to circumvent it, all due to Apollo's curse.

At some point, near the middle of the song, Shawna stopped thinking about the technical demands of the number and the surrounding distractions, and she just became the character. She *was* Cassandra. And when she lowered her head in defeat at the end of the number, the tears falling onto the stage were real.

Bill clapped and hollered, "Brava! Brava!"

*Okay, Dad. I hear you.*

The light cue changed. The musical score shifted to an

ominous drone. Cassandra lifted her head to the gods. The palace doors opened slowly to a dramatic drumbeat, and Cassandra crossed the threshold. The doors closed with a crash. The lights went to black.

## CHAPTER 24

There was a scramble backstage as the actors retreated to their dressing rooms. With only enough time to use the bathroom, change costumes, and touch-up one's makeup, intermissions were over in a flash. Shawna grabbed the water bottle she kept stashed backstage and gulped down half of it. Relief washed over her. She had survived Act One.

When she returned to the dressing room to change her costume, Liz stood before the full-length mirror, straining the seams of her flesh-tone Spanx. Judith was helping Liz into her Act Two costume, a brilliant sapphire blue cloak with silver stars embroidered along the hem. It was another Met Opera donation Judith had refurbished to dramatic effort.

"It's going rather well, don't you think?" Liz asked, eyeing her reflection with a mix of admiration and scrutiny.

"Yes, I think so," replied Shawna, removing her Cassandra wig and placing it on the foam head at her station. "It will be great to have a real audience tomorrow night. It looks like my Dad's the only one out there." Shawna picked up an eyebrow pencil. "Do you think Dudley Wicks will show up tonight?"

"Over my dead body!" Liz snapped. "Wicks wouldn't dare set foot in this theater again, and neither will Penny O'Neil if she knows what's good for her."

Shawna had barely enough time to use the restroom and get her Act Two costume fastened when Blake's voice announced, "Places for Act Two!" over the God-mic. In a flush of nerves, Shawna left the dressing room and joined the rest of the cast backstage.

The flashback of Iphigenia's sacrifice was a powerful, stylized scene showing off both RJ's and Rex's skills. The sequence was designed to impress audiences and critics alike. But of all the scenes, it was the least rehearsed due to the many changes leading up to it.

In a last-minute decision over a bit of stage business, RJ had arranged for a piece of scenery, the sacrificial stone slab, to sink through the stage's trapdoor in a cloud of dry-ice fog after Iphigenia is killed. They hadn't rehearsed it, and Shawna was worried that it wouldn't work, especially considering that she was to lie dead on top of it during this tricky piece of business. Some volunteer stagehand was supposed to help her out of the trap room beneath the floor and escort her back to the stage. All she could do was remind herself this was still a rehearsal and trust that it would all work out somehow.

Katie was cast to play the dead Cassandra in the tableau scene. Katie, wearing a copy of Shawna's Act One costume and wig, took her spot on the turntable behind the main set. They had only marked the scene once before and never with all the stage effects. Further upstage, Bob, playing the dead Agamemnon, was partially concealed behind a column. Agamemnon's billowy red cloak thankfully hid Bob's skinny, varicose veined legs.

The house lights dimmed. Act Two was about to start. Shawna wasn't sure why she felt so nervous. Her difficult parts were done.

Liz brushed past in a rush of taffeta and silk. She stood near the stage right proscenium and dipped her hands in a bucket of fake blood. Then she picked up the large prop knife and rubbed a bit of blood on its tip.

Liz's cue came in the form of ominous drumbeats. She entered with a crazed look, which Shawna thought resembled a campy Norma Desmond in Sunset Boulevard. Liz belted out a dark ballad about sweet revenge while the chorus performed jerky Modernist choreography in pools of red light slightly upstage of her. Clytemnestra's song ended with a dramatic climax timed to the turntable rotating to reveal the murder scene.

Shawna crossed her fingers that the turntable would work. It wobbled a bit at the start of the rotation, and the music barely drowned out the buzz of the motor. Shawna saw Katie trying hard to hold her breath and play dead. Bob looked almost too relaxed. Shawna wondered if he had fallen asleep and might start snoring any minute.

Another clanking sound distracted her. Shawna looked up and gasped at the sight of a slim man crossing the catwalk wearing a black turtleneck and trousers. His shock of thick white hair was a dead giveaway. This was no overhire stagehand. It was Dudley Wicks in the flesh.

"Hutch, look!" Shawna said when her costar appeared at her side. "What the hell is Wicks doing up there?"

"I don't know, but we're on!" Hutch grabbed Shawna's arm and guided her onto the upstage platform. At the end of

Clytemnestra's song, the turntable was supposed to rotate to reveal the flashback sequence. Shawna prayed it would work adequately as she and Hutch found their spots in the dim light. But seeing Wicks on the catwalk had distracted her. Shawna felt around on the set until she located the large altar stone composed of wire, paper mâché, and gray paint over a wooden frame. Lying on her back, she now had a clear view of the catwalk. There was no sign of Wicks. Was it possible she had mistaken an over-hire crew member for the playwright?

Hutch stood over her, getting into his role as Agamemnon, willing to murder his child to appease the gods. Shawna noticed Hutch's dramatic makeup. The thickly painted eyebrows gave his handsome face a severe look. It was perfect for the scene, but it frightened Shawna a bit, especially considering how erratic he had acted toward her. Now, he stood over her with an upraised knife--a prop knife, but still--and a face filled with pure hatred.

*Use it for the scene.*

The tableau scene was nearing the end. Shawna took a deep breath and focused.

The turntable began to move, but Shawna could tell something was wrong. Hutch cursed under his breath as the motor beneath the platform groaned. From the corner of her eye, she spotted Blake in the wings desperately shining a flashlight into the same fuse box that had electrocuted Dougal. Shawna was sure she smelled something burning. Clouds of smoke billowed out from beneath the platform, but it could have been the fog effect.

*It's going to be okay. Just focus on the scene.*

The chorus of Harpies entered the stage. The choreographed *danse macabre* accompanied Shawna as Iphigenia struggled against her father, Agamemnon, attempting to slash her throat. Shawna glanced at the audience, concerned about her Dad's reaction.

Mayor Bill was gone.

*Is the show that bad?*

She gazed up at Hutch. The red lights cast deep shadows into his eyes and open mouth, giving him an eerie resemblance to the tragedy mask Penny had used to terrorize her.

Hutch's arm muscles flexed as he held Shawna against the rock, pressing down hard on her shoulder. They hadn't rehearsed that. He was being too rough with her. Shawna struggled for real. Hutch held her in a firm grip. She jabbed his thigh with her knee.

"Stop," she mumbled under her breath. "You're hurting me!"

The intense music drowned out her words.

The upheld knife began to descend. As she gazed up at the Heavens, her eyes popped open at the sight of a figure flying down from the catwalk wearing a billowy black cape and a grinning comedy mask.

Shawna released a blood-curdling scream, and the entire stage was cloaked in darkness.

"Blake!" RJ shouted from the house. "What's going on?"

There was the sound of someone running across the stage; the platform teeter-tottered, causing everyone to lurch to one side. The chorus of Harpies screamed and scattered. Footsteps hammered across the stage in all directions.

"What's happening? Hey, Blake!" Shawna yelled. The music pounded in her ears.

There was a grunt as Hutch pitched forward, landing heavily on Shawna's chest, pinning her to the altar stone beneath.

"Hutch! Get off me!"

His sticky sweat and makeup dripped onto her face and shoulder.

"I said get off!"

Shawna pushed against Hutch's shoulders with all her might. He groaned and rolled off her, toppling onto the floor. She stood up, her legs tingling, numb. "Blake? What's going on? Hello?"

She figured something had gone wrong with the turntable, causing the lights to blow, and that Blake and RJ were desperately trying to figure out how to fix it. And Wicks, who was fooling around on the catwalk, must have dropped that dummy dressed in the comedy mask just to mess with them.

*But why? What the hell is he trying to prove?*

A metallic clang echoed from above. The work lights flashed on.

Harsh florescent lights bathed the stage in a sickly yellow hue. Shawna sat up on the slab and looked around. Everyone had left the stage except for her and Hutch. Her handsome costar lay curled around the base of the altar stone.

Shawna hopped off the stone slab. "I'm sorry I pushed you, Hutch, but you weren't supposed to fall on me like that. We never rehearsed it that way. Hutch?"

Hutch didn't move.

Shawna crouched down and touched his shoulder. "Hey, Hutch. I'm the one who's supposed to croak in this scene, not you."

Hutch rolled onto his back. His eyes were wide open, gazing upward. Shawna gasped when she saw an open gash in his throat, so wide that she could see the pink column of his trachea. Shawna gazed with amazement at the realistic-looking wound. It appeared as if someone had taken the bucket of fake blood from backstage and poured it over his head as well.

"Is this a joke?" Shawna stood and spun. The black masking curtains billowed in each wing. Beyond that, darkness. Not a sign of life.

Her mind immediately went to the theater pranks that Penny had spoken of, an initiation into the club. Was Shawna the only one who was not in on the joke?

*Of course, they would do it during the final dress rehearsal.*

"Okay, guys, this isn't funny," Shawna hollered out to the empty house. "I get it. You all think I'm too big for my britches, and you need to take me down a peg. Checkmate! You really had me fooled. But can everyone come out now so we can finish the rehearsal?"

Her voice echoed back without a response. Annoyed now, she looked down and saw that there was fake blood on her as well, smearing the front of her white tunic, her arms and hands, and wicking the hem. It looked so real, felt so warm, and it even had the coppery smell that she remembered from the time she had cut her finger badly on one of her Dad's latest culinary gadgets.

Whoever did the makeup job on Hutch was very convincing, but did they have to ruin the costumes, too?

She felt hurt. Betrayed even. Scared. Why was everyone at this theater intent on being so mean to her? What did she ever do but work hard to do her best? Fuck these assholes and their stupid games. She wanted out. She wanted her Dad.

"Hey, Dad!" she cried out. "Don't tell me you're in on it too!"

Shawna's eyes dropped again to Hutch lying still on the floor. His chest wasn't moving, and she wondered how he got his eyes to roll back in his head so that only the whites showed. Fake blood and saliva bubbled on his lips. His skin, where the makeup had begun to wear off, was whiter than white, almost bluish in tone.

Shawna crouched down and shook Hutch's shoulder. "Okay, dude. This is the best acting I've seen you do to date, but enough already. Okay?"

A sour smell reached her nostrils. She realized she was standing in a puddle of Hutch's urine. Repulsed, she jumped back to avoid it. Blood and piss puddled around Hutch's body and moved toward her feet.

*This is no expertly applied makeup and stage effects. This is real!*

With terror running cold through every vein, Shawna faced the empty house and cried out, "Daddy!"

## CHAPTER 25

Something slammed into Shawna from behind, hurling her slight frame to the platform's edge.

Stunned, she lifted her head in time to see the cloaked figure, all in black, with the comedy mask fixed to its face, bow over her with an upraised knife, slick with blood. The exaggerated grin of the comedy mask was more sinister than tragedy had ever looked.

"It's not funny!" Shawna shrieked, striking the attacker in the chest with a two-footed kick. The attacker stumbled backward, and Shawna rolled off the platform. In her rattled brain, she still wanted to believe that it was all a gag, some sick initiation by a group of *artsy-fartsy* weirdos. But there was no denying that Hutch was lying in an expanding pool of blood, and this thing--yes, killer! Was it Penny? Wicks?-- was trying to kill her too.

*This isn't a prank!*

The killer moved toward her, matching her backward pace, step for step. And as Shawna inched toward the edge of the stage in her blood-soaked tunic, she began to laugh hysterically at the situation's absurdity.

The masked killer tilted its head as if confused by Shawna's reaction, its mocking grin mirroring Shawna's panic in a ghastly pantomime.

In a sudden move, the killer gained speed and lunged at her, snapping her out of the hysteria.

Instinct now guiding her, Shawna turned, ran the remaining length of the stage, and leaped into the orchestra pit. Landing hard, she pitched forward, her hands slapping against the floor. Her right leg twisted beneath her. She anticipated the agony of a snapping bone, but she righted herself and stumbled out of the pit.

Hiking up her long, blood-drenched tunic and trailing sash, Shawna bolted down the center aisle. Her right ankle burned with each stride. When she reached the double doors at the back of the house, she turned to look back. The killer had followed her into the pit, landing in a low crouch. Whoever was behind the mask seemed to enjoy toying with her.

Shawna crashed through the double doors and ran into the lobby. The space was empty, lit only by the red exit sign glimmering above the door. Shawna recalled her Dad telling her that public buildings must have doors with push bars that swing out.

*Dad? Where's my Dad?*

She bolted for the door and pushed the bar, anticipating her escape.

She wanted nothing more than to find him and make their escape together, but the door wouldn't budge. She smashed her full weight against the bar. Again, nothing.

Across the lobby were Ron and Harriet's offices, but the lights inside were dim. The doors were probably locked; she couldn't risk trying the doors only to be caught in the open. There was only one option.

Shawna crept through the shadows until she was close enough to step into the box office. It was an obvious hiding place, a temporary respite from terror, but then she remembered the basement door. She crawled toward it and gripped the handle. The double doors at the back of the house creaked open.

With fluttered breath, Shawna twisted the glass knob in her hand and yanked the door. The rapid footsteps of someone running thundered in her ears.

She screamed when the hideous laughing face popped over the counter. The knife stabbed wildly over her head.

Shawna opened the door and squeezed through, slamming it closed just as the masked killer toppled over the counter in hot pursuit.

Shawna fumbled for the latch in the darkness, found a lock on the doorframe, and slid it in place.

She grappled for the string attached to the light. She pulled it, and the fluorescent bulb flickered and buzzed into life. Shawna sat on the top step, panting heavily from the exertion. Cramps filled her sides.

She heard the killer on the other side of the door, matching her breath for breath. The glass knob twisted left and right, then shook violently. Shawna barely had time to catch her breath when she noticed, with alarm, that two screws were missing from the flimsy hardware on the lock. The violent shaking of the old door was starting to loosen the remaining screws.

*If only I had a screwdriver, a tool kit, my Dad!*

Desperate sobs hitched in her throat as Shawna stood and backed down the stairs, eyes trained on the rattling lock.

She reached the concrete floor, desperately circling to find her bearings. Near hysteria, she tried to consciously control her shallow breathing. Slowly, she counted: one, two, three...

She remembered the hurricane doors.

*Once outside, I can run to the highway, flag a car down, get help!*

Galvanized by a solid plan, Shawna bolted for the stairs. Grappling through the cobwebs, she drove her shoulder into the double doors at the top of the stairs.

A rattling chain indicated that a lock had been placed on the other side of the door. Even though she knew it was hopeless, Shawna continued to bang her shoulder into the door until she was sobbing and exhausted, and pain flamed through her tired muscles.

With no other option, Shawna backed down the steps and began searching through the dusty piles of junk for any tool she could use as a weapon. All the while, the incessant pounding on the basement door continued.

The basement door crashed open.

With nowhere else to go, Shawna plunged into the basement's vast darkness, running blindly into a maze of scenery and sticks of old furniture. The only light was an occasional daylight window where dim moonlight drifted in.

A scream caught in her throat as she crashed into an old dress form in her path. Her bruised legs ached with new pain, but the dress form gave her an idea.

She dug her fingernails into the skirt of her costume, found the hem, and ripped off the bottom half. She undid the long red sash, stiff with Hutch's drying blood, and draped it over the dress form. She then ripped the wig off her head and placed it on the neck stump just as the figure appeared in a pool of moonlight streaming through one of the high basement windows. The cloaked figure stopped and cocked its head to one side as if listening.

Using the darkness to her advantage, Shawna, now wearing only a short tunic, her hair concealed beneath a wig cap, sank slowly to the floor and crab-crawled backward to hide behind a lawn mower. She watched the killer move cautiously into the darkness. The gasoline smell from the mower was overpowering. Shawna swallowed a sneeze and dug down deeper into the cubbyhole of darkness.

The killer continued to advance slowly on the dress form. A flash of a car's headlights passed over one of the windows. The killer jumped out of the light into the shadows. Shawna slapped her hand over her mouth to keep from calling out. More than ever, she wanted her Dad. She prayed he had left during the performance because he had been called away.

*Maybe he had to leave but returned, and now he's searching for me. But how will he ever find me down here?*

The killer emerged from the shadows. The headlights passed over the window again, illuminating the dress form. The killer lunged for it. The dress form toppled backward with a crash, and the killer fell on top of it. Shawna watched in horror as the killer straddled the dress form and, gripping the knife's hilt with two hands, repeatedly drove the blade into it in a frenzied attack.

Seeing her chance to escape, Shawna leaped to her feet. Unburdened by her heavy costume, she ran faster now. Doubling back, she sprinted toward the staircase, trying to avoid the dark objects obscuring her path. She reached the pool of florescent light near the washing machine. Slapping footsteps were quickly advancing on her.

She reached the stairs, but halfway up, the knife emerged from between the staircase treads with a frenzied stabbing motion. The smiling golden face peeked up at her with mocking menace. The knife's point slashed at Shawna's ankles, slicing through the laces of one sandal. Shawna kicked it loose into the killer's mask and bolted up the remaining stairs. She squeezed through the tiny door, slid under the counter, flew across the lobby, and crashed through the double doors into the house.

"Help!" she screamed, running down the aisle. "Someone's trying to kill me! I need help! Please! Is anybody there?"

She ran up the side stairs onto the stage. Hutch's body still lay on the platform. His mouth gaped open grotesquely. One eye stared blindly, while the other was closed and slack. The blood around him had begun to congeal. Her lungs burning, she circled the stage.

*I need to escape, but how?*

She recalled the backdoor, which Blake kept propped open. She prayed the paint can was still there.

Shawna slipped through the gap in the upstage curtain and stumbled through scenery and pulley ropes until she reached the back wall. She felt her way along the cool bricks till she reached the doorjamb. Her bare foot banged into the paint can. It was there, but inside the door. She tried the door. Locked.

As her heart sank, Shawna recalled how her Mom and Dad would fight when she was a child. She had blocked out so much to paint the perfect family in her mind, but it wasn't always ideal. And when they'd fight, little Shawna would make herself as small as possible, squeezing into the darkest corner of her closet until the storm had passed.

She did the same now, sliding down the wall and wrapping her arms around her knees till she was as small and tight as a ball. Her pursuer's feet appeared in the gap between the curtain and the floor, pacing back and forth.

There was a sound of a door slamming near stage right. The feet beneath the curtain took off in that direction.

Part of Shawna wanted to stay curled up like a ball forever, but she wasn't a child anymore, and she couldn't hide from the truth of what was happening, just like she couldn't hide from the reality of her parents' fragile marriage. She straightened to her full height, then reached down and unlaced her other sandal. It was hard running with only one shoe.

Her head was aching from the tight wig cap. She yanked it off and tossed it aside, letting her wild curls loose. Slowly, she inched her way along the back wall until she reached the stage left wing. She had a good view of the stage now. For the first time, she noticed that Katie and Bob were still in their spots on the upstage portion of the platform.

With pity in her heart, Shawna stepped onto the platform and approached Bob. The poor old guy was lying on his stomach just as RJ had instructed him to do, but there was no mistaking that he was dead. A pool of blood surrounded him; there was no sign of life in his bluish-pale skin. Shawna backed away from the gruesomeness.

A hand reached out and grabbed her ankle.

"Don't scream," whispered Katie from the floor, her fingers desperately digging into Shawna's flesh.

Nearly fainting from the jolt of adrenaline coursing through her body, Shawna recovered and crouched down, whispering, "Katie. Thank God. Are you hurt?"

"Just-just my shoulder." Katie released Shawna's ankle and groaned. "I've been playing dead, hoping someone would help."

"Katie, stay with me. We're both going to get out of here." She helped the teen rise to her feet. Blood poured from the slash on Katie's shoulder. Shawna whipped off the veil from around Katie's neck and held it against the wound.

"Apply pressure," Shawna said. "Okay?"

Katie nodded weakly.

Shawna tried to appear calm for Katie's sake, but she was far from confident. Her gaze bounced to each cardinal point, trying to determine which was the safest route to take. There were fire exit doors on each side of the house. The killer could have neglected to lock one of them. Katie leaned heavily against Shawna's shoulder, her head limp.

"Katie," Shawna said. "Do you think you can walk off the stage into the house? I think we can get to one of those exit doors."

"I'll try." Katie righted herself.

Shawna decided that being out in the open was probably the best strategy. Being able to see the killer--it had to be Penny!--approaching would give them a better chance of escape. Finding a hiding place was also an option, but Penny knew the theater better than Shawna and she would use that to her advantage.

Shawna guided Katie slowly through the set's palace doors. The stage and house were dark, lit only by the red exit signs and the spill of the catwalk lights, which created a shadowy grid pattern on the floor.

They hadn't traveled far downstage when Katie collapsed and Shawna crumpled under her weight.

"Shit." Shawna set Katie down on the altar stone, thinking that if she left her on the floor then she might not be able to pull her up again. She moved her lips close to Katie's ear and whispered, "Wait here. I'm going to check the doors."

"Don't leave me!" Katie clung desperately to Shawna's wrists.

"I'll be right back."

As Shawna forced herself away, Katie's grip loosened; her hand fell limply to one side of the altar stone. Shawna looked down at the suffering teen, noting how much she appeared like a virgin sacrifice in her costume and wig, covered in blood. But this wasn't the theater; this was real life, but the reality of it seemed impossible to compute.

A clang on the catwalk jangled her nerves. She glanced up but saw nothing except the dimly lit grid, heavy sandbags, rope, and thick wires attached to hanging lamps.

*Is Penny watching me now, planning her next attack?*

Fighting the lingering pain in her legs and side, Shawna moved cautiously to the right side of the stage, down the stairs and side aisle. She was now only a few short steps away from the door. The glowing red exit sign radiated as a beacon of hope.

With a prayer on her lips, Shawna pressed against the door's metal bar and pushed. It seemed like a miracle when the door swung open. Warm summer air floated in, and Shawna breathed in the sweat smell of grass and freedom.

Her heart sang as she gazed at the natural scene: the low mist clinging to the ground, fireflies lighting up the distant cornfield, and the full moon hovering over the willow tree. Shawna wanted to escape into that vision like the children jumping into the pictures in the Mary Poppins movie.

*I could leave and get help, or I can--damn!*

Shawna glanced back at the stage where Katie still lay, helpless on the altar stone.

*We're both getting out of here!*

Shawna ran back down the side aisle toward the stage. But just as her bare feet hit the first step, a spotlight illuminated the altar stone. The blast of bright light caused Katie to stir.

"Shawna?" Katie sat up and looked about, perplexed by what was happening. She clutched her wounded shoulder and grimaced from the pain.

"Katie!" Shawna shouted from the edge of the stage. "The side door is open. Come on! We need to go now!"

Katie swung her legs around the front of the altar stone. "Shawna?"

"Katie, I'm right here on the side steps. Let's go!"

Katie screamed when the altar stone began to sink into the trapdoor. A cloud of dry ice fog shot out from beneath it.

"Katie, jump!" Shawna screamed.

"Shawna!"

The stone sank with Katie on it. Shawna ran across the stage, and leaped onto the platform, but the fog and lights blinded her. She fumbled about in confusion until she tripped over Hutch's robe. She pitched forward, landing on his body.

She shuddered at the coolness of Hutch's flesh, the disgusting aroma of blood and gore. His limbs had already begun to stiffen. Revolted, Shawna raised her head in time to watch Katie being sucked into the floor.

"Katie, no!"

Shawna crawled on hands and knees until she reached the spot. But by that time, the trapdoor had closed. Katie was gone.

## CHAPTER 26

Her only thought now was to get out and get help, in that order. Shawna ran back across the stage, flew down the steps and up the aisle, and rammed against the side door.

It opened to someone standing on the threshold: a large, robed figure silhouetted by cool moonlight. Shawna screamed as an arm reached out and shoved her back inside.

"Liz!" Shawna cried when she saw who it was.

"Thank God," Liz panted. Still dressed in the regal garb of Clytemnestra, Liz had lost her wig during the course of the night's madness, and now her black hair was coiled around her face like Medusa's snakes. "I went to get something from my car during intermission and I've been locked outside ever since. What the hell is going on in here? Where's RJ?"

"I don't know," Shawna said. "But we need to get out of here. Penny has gone insane. She killed Hutch and Bob, and she's trying to kill me too."

Liz stared at Shawna, taking in her disheveled appearance, her bloodstained costume. "Are you nuts?"

Shawna burst into tears. "Liz, we have to get out of here!"

"I'm not going anywhere until I find RJ."

"But--"

"Oh, there he is." Liz waved at a shadow moving inside the booth at the back of the house. Lifting her skirts, she started up the aisle.

"Liz!" Shawna shouted after her. "It's not safe! Please!"

Ignoring Shawna's pleas, Liz headed for the door in the far corner at the back of the house leading to the booth.

Shawna hovered on the threshold between the stuffy dark theater and the misty night with its summer music of crickets and bullfrogs.

*I can't leave Liz.*

Fighting against her own survival instinct, Shawna raced up the aisle toward the booth. If RJ was in the booth, she could warn them both. Then--

"Liz, run!" Shawna shouted when the killer rose from the back row and moved toward Liz with an upraised knife.

Liz reeled back in surprise, took several stumbling steps backward as the blade descended in a sweeping arc, plunging deep into the cleavage of her breasts. Incomprehensible babble and blood fountained from Liz's mouth. Shawna clamped her hands over her ears to blot out the horrible noise. The knife remained in the killer's hand as Liz sank to the floor with a prolonged groan.

Shawna stepped backward toward the side door. The killer looked up, straightened, and walked toward Shawna, matching her steps.

The exaggerated grin of the comedy mask, now spattered with Liz's blood, mocked Shawna's terror. Shawna stumbled over her own feet as she continued her backward crawl toward the door.

"Penny, please," Shawna begged, although her words sounded shallow, desperate, not fooling anyone, least of all herself. "You need help. I can get you help."

The horrible, mocking face moved closer, hypnotizing Shawna with its empty gaze, its hideous grin. Shawna was only a few feet from the door. Why couldn't she will herself to turn and bolt to freedom?

Laughter rippled through the comedy mask. The killer lunged toward her. Shawna screamed and ducked. The killer jumped in Shawna's path, blocking the door. The knife arced through the air, aimed straight for Shawna's throat. Shawna sidestepped it and escaped through a row of seats. The killer pursued her. Shawna ran to the back of the house. Liz said RJ was in the booth.

*But why isn't he helping us?*

Shawna pounced on the door at the back of the house, swung it open, then slammed it shut behind her just in time to see the killer lurching forward.

She found a lock, slid it into place and sank onto the stairs, limp with relief. She dropped her head in her hands, tried to hold it together.

*Don't crumble now. People need help.*

Cold sweat flushed through her pores. As she caught her breath, the true horror of what she had witnessed, the brutal murder of Liz, took shape in her mind.

Part of her still clung to the hope that this was all just one long, elaborate prank performed by the world's best acting troupe. Their talent for creating verisimilitude and *mise-en-scène* would go down in history as the greatest theater hoax of all time, and Shawna would laugh about it one day. She might have to spend some time recovering in a padded cell first, but she'd laugh.

*RJ will tell me the truth. That this whole night is an awful, terrible, nightmarish gag!*

Shawna half-crawled up the stairs to the booth. She recalled being shown the small room with the black walls on her first day and feeling intimidated by the equipment with all the levers and buttons. There was another door at the top of the stairs directly leading to the booth. She gripped the handle and cautiously opened the door.

She discovered RJ seated on a high stool, fiddling with the levers on the light board. He was slumped forward and didn't seem to notice when Shawna entered.

"RJ?" Her voice was a child's, trembling and terrified.

RJ looked up at her with a dazed expression. An empty bottle of Cutty Sark rolled off the counter and landed with a thud on top of a man lying on the floor. His black clothes blended into the dark carpeting, but his shock of white hair confirmed that it was Dudley Wicks, lying facedown and not moving a muscle.

"Who is it?" asked RJ. His words were slurred. "Who's there?"

Shawna leaned against the wall, trembling. "It's-it's Shawna."

A smile of recognition broke the dam of confusion on RJ's face. His drunk, unfocused eyes looked her up and down. "Hello, Shawna. I'd offer you a drink, but I'm afraid it's gone, e-v-e-r-y last drop."

"RJ, we need to leave. Do you have keys for any of these exit doors?"

"Exit doors?" Frowning deeply, he shook his head. "You'll have to ask Blake about that."

"Do you know where Blake is?"

"Nope. Everybody left." His chin wobbled, and a string of drool trickled onto his beard. "Everyone abandoned me and my beautiful dream."

Suppressing a sob, RJ went back to fiddling with the light board. Through the window in the booth, Shawna watched the colored spots and patterns dancing on the stage as he slid the levers up and down.

Shawna pressed against the wall to avoid Wick's body. "RJ, do you have your phone on you?"

"My what?"

"Your cell phone." At the start of the rehearsal, Blake had collected all the actors' phones and put them in a "safe place," wherever that was.

"Phone. No." RJ gazed back at the stage. "I don't like new technology." He took a deep breath, exhaled slowly. "I was born in the wrong era, Shawna. I would have been happy at the Old Vic or the Lyceum, treading the boards with the likes of Wilde and Irving. Today's world is crap!"

Realizing she was getting nowhere with RJ, Shawna crouched down and, fighting back revulsion, began to dig through Wicks' pockets. His body was already cold.

RJ looked down at her. "What the hell are you doing with him?"

"I'm looking for a phone." Tears of terror and frustration were flowing now. Shawna didn't try to stop them.

"Why?" he barked.

"So, I can call the cops!"

RJ rose from the stool. Towering over her, he boomed, "Why do you want to do that?"

"Because--" She pointed a trembling finger at Wicks. "Penny killed him--she's gone crazy and killed everyone. Don't you know what's happening?"

"Penny!" RJ laughed hoarsely. "Penny didn't kill this

motherfucker, I did!" RJ drew back his leg and kicked the side of Wicks' head. Shawna winced and backed away in horror.

"And I'd do it again if I had to. He came here tonight, dressed like some cat burglar, and tried to ruin my play!" RJ pointed toward the stage. "First, he's up on the catwalk fucking around with the lights. Then, while Blake was fixing the turntable backstage, I discovered him in the booth messing with all the cues. It was his fault Dougal died. He almost got us shut down, but he can't hurt us anymore."

"H-how did you?"

"Kill him?"

RJ turned to her and grinned. "Shawna, my dear, I never leave home without my Dover Thrift edition of *Hamlet* or my antique Derringer." He pulled a small silver pistol from his tweed sport coat and casually waved it at her. "This is the gun I used when I played John Wilkes Booth at the Wilbur in Boston. It's an exact replica of the gun that killed Lincoln. We used blanks in the production, of course, but I don't think the prop man knew that this damn thing actually worked." He gazed at it admiringly. "I find it small but effective, just like you." He took a step forward, pinning her with his drunken glare.

"I think you have what it takes to be an actress: raw talent, that goes without saying. Pretty, a bit short in stature, but when did that ever stop the likes of Bernhardt or La Duse, or the great Judy Garland for that matter?" He shook his head sadly. "The greatest artists always suffer the most." He turned his head to look at Wicks in disgust. "And there's always some prick trying to fuck it up and stab you in the back!" Spit flew from RJ's lips as he spoke. He seemed to have the face of an old man, old and bitter and insane!

Shawna moved toward the door. "I'm sure Wicks threatened you and your show, and that's why you..."

RJ shrugged. "He may have. I honestly don't remember. But, Shawna, I want you to understand that I had to do it. I had no choice."

"Uh-huh." She felt the doorknob in her hand.

"It was imperative to my work." He moved toward her.

"I understand."

He took another step. "Nothing is more sacred."

When RJ was almost on top of her, Shawna flung open the door. She started back at the sight of Rex running up the stairs.

"Shawna, RJ--thank God you're--"

Before Rex could finish, RJ fired the gun. Shawna screamed as Rex groaned and toppled backward down the stairs.

RJ pushed past Shawna, shouting, "Out of my way, you ungrateful fools! I have a theater to run!" He staggered down the steps, trampling over Rex who had curled into a tight fetal position, softly groaning. Shawna moved down the steps toward him.

"Oh my God, Rex!"

Rex was still alive, but his breath was raspy and shallow. Shawna could tell he was in shock. "I-I fell asleep in one of the offices. When I woke up, everyone was gone." He licked his lips and tried to say more but couldn't.

"Rex, do you have a phone?"

Rex gazed at her with confusion before he nodded. The simple movement of his head seemed to cause intense pain.

She leaned over Rex. "Is it in one of your pockets?"

He shook his head and winced. "In my bag downstairs." Shawna could tell that it was too much effort for Rex to speak. He shut his eyes tightly.

"Downstairs in the house, where you were sitting before?"

Rex nodded weakly.

Shawna jumped to her feet. "Hold on, Rex. I'll be right back."

She scurried past him, careful not to touch him and cause more pain. When she reached the bottom of the stairs, she opened the door a crack and peered out into the house. All she saw were the backs of empty theater seats.

Just hours ago, her Dad had sat in the second row. Where did he go? Then, a thought crept into her mind, more terrifying than anything she had witnessed during this dreadful night.

*What if Penny had killed him, too?*

He alluded to some dealings with her in one of their earlier conversations. Shawna sensed he was holding back-- perhaps that business with the doctor. Did Penny have a reason to silence him?

The thought nearly drowned her in despair, but she swam above the current. She was Mayor Bill's daughter, after all, and he'd raised her to be intelligent and rational, to have grit and courage. Now, all she had to do was step away from the door, travel about twenty feet to where Rex had been sitting earlier that night and retrieve his phone.

Sucking in a deep breath, Shawna bravely slipped through the door. Crouching low, she crept to the center aisle. Before she could reach Rex's seat she heard anguished weeping. Gazing down the side aisle, she saw RJ bent over Liz's body. He was wailing softly and mumbling incomprehensibly, his body shaking with sobs.

The sight pained Shawna, but she couldn't take in the scene for too long. She had to get to Rex's phone and call for help! She hoped some of the cast and crew had made it to safety. But if they had, wouldn't someone have called the police already?

She cocked an ear to the double doors when she passed the lobby entrance, listening for any stirrings there. No sound. Keeping low, she scanned the rows but found nothing but folded-up seats.

*What the hell happened to Rex's bag?*

She started moving row by row toward the stage when RJ abruptly stood, like a soldier from a foxhole.

The killer stood before him.

RJ lowered his gun with a bitter chuckle. "Oh, it's you!" His voice dripped with contempt. "And to think I've put up with you all these years. I must have been out of my mind. I knew you were a jealous fool, but was it really necessary to murder my wi--"

With a banshee wail, the killer leaped on top of RJ. They both crashed to the floor. The gun flew from RJ's hands. When he tried to retrieve it, the killer brought the knife overhead and plunged it into RJ's back. He groaned and fell on his face. Shawna stood transfixed as the figure stood over RJ, repeatedly driving the knife into his back as he twitched and groaned, arms and legs paddling helplessly.

Clamping a hand over her mouth to keep from screaming, Shawna crouched behind the last seat in the row.

*One advantage of being small is I can hide. Oh, dear God. Let me hide.*

Shawna flinched at the sound of footsteps moving toward her accompanied by the slapping noise as each seat was flipped up.

As the killer approached, Shawna realized she had only two choices left: stay curled in a ball and hide or run like hell!

## CHAPTER 27

The only thing she had left was instinct. Yielding to it, Shawna jumped to her feet and bolted toward the stage. When she reached the orchestra pit, she saw that RJ was not only still alive but crawling down the side aisle like a snail, leaving a bloody stream in his wake.

"I must," RJ croaked. "I must die on stage. Help me, please..."

Shawna stole a glance up the side aisle. The killer was advancing, moving quickly toward her with an upraised knife.

"I'm sorry, RJ. I'm sorry." she mumbled.

He reached out as she rushed past.

Leaving RJ behind, she scrambled onto the stage via the stage right stairway. She skirted around the single spotlight and passed through the wing toward the dressing rooms. She collided with the Genie in the dark. It was fully extended to the light grid. For a wild moment she considered climbing it. But when she looked up, she almost screamed when she saw Blake's body hanging upside down by one foot from the Genie's platform. Blake's eyes were open, staring at nothing. Shawna was transfixed by Blake's body. She stood there as large clots of Blake's blood rained down, striking Shawna's face.

*My, God! Is everyone dead?*

She glanced back at the stage. The killer slashed through the stage right curtain in pursuit of her.

Shawna ran to the women's dressing room, trying to recall if there was a lock on the door, a phone, or a window through which she could squeeze. She opened the door a crack, slipped through, and closed it. Shawna felt desperately for a lock, but there was none. The makeup lights framing each mirror blazed hot. She nearly shrieked in terror when she saw her own reflection staring back at her with wild hair and panting like an injured animal. Never had she looked so pale, and the smeared makeup around her eyes created a ghastly effect. The blood on her white costume had turned a foul brown color.

"Judith," she whispered, tearing her gaze from the reflection.

Rapid footsteps thundered past the door. Shawna clamped her hands over her mouth, careful not to make a sound. She had just released a sigh of relief when she heard the footsteps stop, then backpedal toward the dressing room.

*God, no!*

Shawna retreated to the only refuge left: the bathroom. She entered and shut the door. With trembling fingers she hooked the flimsy latch. Only after she was calm enough to breathe did she notice the bathroom was filled with clouds of thick fog. It coated the mirror above the sink. Someone had left the shower running.

Shawna heard the dressing room door slam open. She backed toward the shower. She kept her gaze focused on the bathroom door. The knob turned. Shawna desperately searched the bathroom for any kind of weapon. If only there was a straight razor in the shabby medicine cabinet over the sink.

The lock rattled, and Shawna observed with horror as the knife poked through the gap around the doorframe and flicked at the lock. The knife tip was still wet and stained with Liz's and RJ's blood. Each flick of the blade edged the lock's hook a tiny bit higher. The vinyl shower curtain pressed into Shawna's back.

The room was steamy. Her bare feet slipped on the wet tiles. A foul smell tickled her nostrils. Shawna turned and gagged on the scream that caught in her throat.

Judith sat slumped in the corner of the shower stall in an ocean of blood, legs splayed, head tilted forward. Her prized dressmaking shears were open, the blades thrust to the hilt in each of Judith's eyes.

The latch gave and the door flung open. The steam from the shower obscured the figure on the threshold.

Shawna screamed with terror, gripped the scissors and pulled them from Judith's eyes, releasing a bloody, gelatinous goo and repulsive squishing sound.

Shawna grunted as she barreled forward, thrusting the scissors wildly at the killer in the doorway. She felt the contact when the shears hit bone, sending a shock wave up the length of her arm.

Releasing the scissors, Shawna scrambled over the killer, who was now slumped in a dark heap on the floor.

Shawna ran mindlessly from the dressing room, only slowing down when she recognized the dim corridor leading to the bowels of the barn where the old scenery was stored and the cow cages still smelled of straw and manure.

The cow! The *Gypsy* cow marked the spot where she'd

find the old wooden ladder leading to the hayloft. There was a sliding door up there leading to freedom. The killer wouldn't think to lock that door. Perhaps if she hung onto the edge then the jump wouldn't be far enough to kill her, just break her leg maybe.

*And then what? Lie on the ground with a broken leg, waiting for the killer to show up and finish me off?*

A loud bang echoed down the hallway. The killer was still alive!

Exhausted, Shawna staggered forward, bare feet on rough wooden planks, inviting splinters.

Turning a dark corner, she collided with the cow's head. It toppled off the trunk covered in Vaudeville stickers and rolled onto the floor. Shawna stumbled into something wet. She looked down and saw a trail of blood leading to the cow's head. Afraid, yet not able to stop herself, she approached the cow with its garish smile and long black lashes above moveable eyes.

Those eyes rolled back as if they were alive when Shawna slowly lifted the head. It was heavier than she had expected. In a moment, she knew why.

Ron's severed head dropped from the neck opening and thumped to the floor at Shawna's feet. The neck had been roughly sawed, the trachea was exposed, and the blood--so much blood.

Shawna screamed and scrambled to get away from the horror. The horrifying object rolled toward her as if was still animated. The toupee fixed itself to the floor with a bloody glue. The top of Ron's head was bald and shiny. She half expected the mouth to move, to call her Eve again and mock her. For a moment, Shawna thought the head did speak.

"Eve, little miss evil," it whispered.

*No! No! That's in my mind.*

Shawna backed up onto the ladder. Ron's head watched her with milky eyes as if criticizing her decision. But there seemed no other option than to climb. Shawna pulled herself up the first rung, then the second. The adrenaline produced by fear was slowly draining from her body. Daggers of fatigue pierced her lungs. It took every bit of energy left inside her to climb and climb.

She reached the second floor. Nothing but darkness confronted her.

Hand over hand, Shawna made it to the third story. She crawled off the last rung and onto the floor. Fumbling through the darkness, she found the far wall and the edge of the sliding door. Palming the rough-hewn door for support, she stood and thrust her weight against it. The rusted wheels above the door complained and barely moved an inch. Shawna tried again and again, groaning with the effort, until there was just enough space for her to squeeze through.

As if she'd just turned the page of an old dusty book to reveal a brilliant picture panorama, Shawna gazed at the full moon hanging high in the starry sky. A cool breeze lifted her hair and tingled her damp skin. The scent of honeysuckle wafted over the distant fields and fed her soul with freedom's sweet perfume.

*Can I do it? Can I jump?*

Shawna sank to the floor. She couldn't do it, couldn't hurl herself into that beckoning night. Her tiny frame shuddered with sobs. Dizziness and fatigue conquered her at last. The curtain fell.

Shawna awoke to a symphony of sweet birdsong. Her eyelids fluttered open gently to a pastoral tableau of dewy fields shimmering with morning sunlight. The willow tree branches swayed in the soft breeze, stirring up the scent of grass, honeysuckle, and wild strawberries.

She had made it through the night. She had survived.

There was a rusted chain attached to the wall beside her. She used it to help her slowly rise to her feet, then she stood like a new-born foal on wobbly legs. She gripped the chain and gazed at the parking lot below. The lot was empty except for a black luxury SUV coated with morning dew.

*Dad's car!*

The vision of the black SUV filled Shawna with renewed strength. The problem of getting out of the hayloft wasn't as insurmountable as it had been in the dead of night. The heavy chain bolted to the wall looked strong enough to support her weight. And among the jumble of costumes, she was bound to find some rope, or she could make some out of some of the old robes, weave them together to make it strong.

Galvanized by fresh hope, Shawna went to work. In the flood of sunlight spilling through the open hayloft door, Shawna poked around the ramshackle space, careful not to step on a rusty nail, although death by tetanus was preferable to death by a maniac's blade. She paused to listen for any noise floating up from below. The barn was as quiet as if abandoned, with only the occasional creak of timber, scuttle of pigeons on the roof, or buzzing carpenter bees.

A length of clothesline presented itself, one end attached to a support beam by a rusty nail, the other trailing to the floor. Shawna picked up the clothesline and yanked it hard. The nail flew off the beam and pinged off somewhere.

Excited, reminding herself with every breath to slow

down and do it right, Shawna knotted the nylon rope every few feet, then double, triple, quadruple-knotted the end of the rope to the rusted chain.

She had learned how to rappel down a rock wall at summer camp when she was twelve. She'd need gloves. After toppling over a few moldering cardboard boxes marked "Ladies Accessories," she found a pair of black leather ones. The vintage gloves were tiny, but Shawna managed to squeeze her hands into them, and then there she was, on the razor's edge, poised in the open hayloft door, the sunlight bathing her with energy and hope. She dropped the rope and watched it snake toward the ground. It didn't quite reach all the way, but it was close enough.

She imagined how she might look to someone randomly passing by: a Hellish version of Wonder Woman in her bloodstained tunic and breastplate.

She took a breath and descended the side of the barn. The leather gloves helped tremendously, as did the small gaps between the warping barn boards where her bare feet could find purchase. Never had she been so aware of her body's weight, the pull of gravity ready to snatch her with one false move.

*One step at a time. Keep your balance, and don't let go!*

She reached the final knot in the rope and jumped the last several feet to the ground. The hard gravel cut into her tender feet. She fell back on her butt. The freed rope undulated above her like a cat's tail.

*I did it! I'm free! Now, to find my Dad.*

Shawna's thoughts were disturbed by a pitiful voice cutting through the dense morning air.

"Help me, please. Oh, please help."

Shawna spun around to see Harriet struggling to maneuver her wheelchair through the theater's lobby door.

As Shawna rushed to help her, she noticed that Harriet was bleeding from a shoulder wound. Harriet's salt and pepper hair hung loosely and her eyeglasses were gone. In the morning sunlight, Shawna realized that Harriet was much younger than she had initially thought, she was more like her Dad's age.

"Harriet, are you all right?" Shawna gripped the handles of the wheelchair and yanked it over the threshold. "Is there anyone else alive in there?"

Harriet shook her head weakly. "They got Ron, everybody. Got me, too. I'm bleeding."

"My Dad's car is right over there," Shawna said, pointing at the SUV. "There's a police radio inside. We can break the window if we have to."

It took effort to wheel Harriet across the lot; Shawna was winded by the time they reached the car. She didn't expect it to be unlocked, and God knows where her Dad was, hopefully alive. Hopefully--

She pulled at the passenger-side door handle, and the door swung open. Penny was curled up in the front seat, a black robe covering her body and the bronze tragedy mask resting beside her. Bill was in the driver's seat, reclining, his head thrown back and his mouth was agape.

## CHAPTER 28

Her Dad wasn't dead. He was snoring.

Shawna froze, trying to process the twisted tableau before her. Penny blinked at the sunlight flooding into the vehicle, yawned, and sat up. It took Penny a moment to recognize Shawna.

"Oh, it's you," Penny said. She flipped down the visor and fluffed out her hair. She licked her finger and rubbed it beneath her eyes where her mascara had smeared.

Bill stirred, sat up with a blank look, and then swung his gaze at Shawna.

"What time is it?" he mumbled. "Shawna, thank God you're all right. What's wrong? Why are you looking at me like that?"

Penny laughed and leaned against Bill's chest. "Can't you see your daughter is freaked out to find us together. Well, as you can see, it's true. We've been lovers for quite a while. Haven't we, babe?"

Bill shuffled in his seat, raked his hand through his hair and gazed sheepishly at Shawna. "Honey, I wanted to tell you when the time was right. I-I want you to know that no woman could possibly replace your mother."

Penny darted a dirty look in Bill's direction. "What's that's supposed to mean?"

Shawna slowly backed away from the door. "Y-you." She pointed at the black robe and tragedy mask. "You killed all of them and you--" She swung her finger accusingly at her Dad. "You were in on it."

Penny rolled her eyes. "In on what? Yeah, I wore that stupid mask and robe to prank you that one time! It was your Dad's idea. He wanted to scare you away from the theater, to get this place closed down for good so he could get his real estate investment off the ground."

Penny nudged Bill with her elbow. "Tell her the truth, babe. I came back tonight to scare you again and we both got locked out. Believe me, the last thing I wanted to do was spend the night in this cramped car."

Shawna noticed how her Dad couldn't hold her gaze. Her head swam with confusion.

"Why aren't you saying anything, Bill?" Penny whined. "This was all your idea, remember?"

Penny shifted her hostile gaze back at Shawna. "It's about time you knew all about me and your Dad." Penny grinned widely at Bill. "I'm going to be her new step-mother. Right, Daddy?"

"Stepmother?" Shawna stepped back in shock.

"Hey, honey. You look really shook up. I can explain." Bill opened the driver's side door and climbed out. He skirted around the hood of the car.

"Christ, it's hot in here." Penny slid out of the open passenger door and stepped onto the grass.

Bill approached his daughter, sweating and disheveled. He opened his arms wide as if pleading for understanding.

"I'm sorry I ruined your play. Penny and I never wanted anyone to get hurt, especially you."

Shawna at last found her voice amidst the confusion. "But people are hurt, Dad. And most of them are dead, and she killed them!" Repulsed, scared, Shawna stepped back and stumbled over Harriet's wheelchair. In her shock at discovering her Dad with Penny, she'd forgotten all about the poor injured lady who needed help.

Harriet's wheelchair was empty.

"She was right here," Shawna said. "Where did she go?"

"Who?" Bill asked.

"Harriet." Shawna spun all the way around. The sun was fully up now, baking the top of her head, making her dizzy.

Penny stretched and wandered into the shade of the willow tree. "Babe, can we please get out of here?" She spoke with an exaggerated baby voice. "I need my bweckfast."

As Penny settled on the grass, picking a random dandelion, a robed figure wearing the comedy mask emerged from behind the willow tree at her back.

Penny glared at Shawna. "What is your problem now."

"It's, it's..." Shawna's words died on her lips. She could only point and stare.

Penny turned toward the figure just as the knife plunged into her chest.

"Dad!" Shawna screamed.

Bill rushed toward the killer, but it was too late. By the time he had knocked the figure to the ground and wrestled the knife from its grip, Penny was dead. The killer lay supine on the grass. Bill threw the bloody knife into the weeds.

"Oh, God. Penny!" Bill mumbled, kneeling over Penny's lifeless body. "We need to call for help." He clambered to his feet.

"Dad!" Shawna screamed when the killer began to stir.

Bill clocked it with a hard right punch, knocking away the grinning mask. The face that remained beneath the grotesque visage was one that no one expected.

"Harriet!" Shawna cried.

Harriet lay on the grass, her silver hair spread about her face. Her glassy eyes gazed up at Bill. Blood poured from her mouth; the sickly grin on her face rivaled any Halloween jack-o-lantern horror.

Shawna looked back at the wheelchair. "I don't understand."

Harriet licked the blood from her lips and widened her grin into the folds of her cheeks. "Your father understands." She began to laugh, then coughed and gripped her shoulder.

Shawna realized it was Harriet whom she had injured in the dressing room with Judith's shears, Harriet who had done all that carnage wearing the comedy mask. "Why, Harriet? Why did you do it?"

Bill looked down at the injured woman on the grass, his expression grim. "This isn't Harriet," he said. "Harriet Harman doesn't exist."

"Then who is--"

"Shawna," Bill's lip curled with disgust. "Meet Candace Laherty."

"What?"

A look of smug satisfaction replaced Candace's grin. "That's right, Shawna. Over twenty years ago, your father and I were lovers. He broke it off with me because your mother was pregnant with you. But he would have dumped me eventually. With what little self-esteem I had left, I came here." Her eyes glanced off the theater barn. "If I failed at life, I could at least succeed in the world of pretend." Her chin trembled, the corners of her mouth turned down. "But

I failed at that too. So, I decided to end it all. But your Dad, the big hero, showed up and rescued me. I was hurt, partially paralyzed. He took me to a hospital over the river. While I recovered, he got me a new identity and a new life. While you were growing up, he supported me financially, anything to keep me quiet so I wouldn't stain the reputation of Tullytown's rising star."

Shawna turned to Bill. "Dad? Say something. Is what she's saying true?"

Bill looked away, the truth of Candace's speech written plainly on his guilty face.

Candace coughed and continued, "Your father's bad conscience was my ticket to a new life. I applied for the job at the theater and got it. He was incensed, but what could he do about it? What would the town think of their precious Mayor with his perfect family? So, I worked in this theater for decades, and none of those fools even recognized poor Candace Laherty." She winced from the pain in her wound.

"Dad, she needs help." Shawna looked at her father. His hands were clenched into tight fists.

"Look at him," Candace croaked. "He'd rather see me bleed to death than have to face the truth about himself. How many women in this town did you screw, Mr. Mayor?"

"Dad. I'm going to call for an ambulance on the police radio."

"No." Bill clutched Shawna's arm. "Let her finish. I want to hear it all. I want you to hear it too. You have as much right as anyone to know the truth."

Candace turned her head to one side and coughed up blood and phlegm. The color in her cheeks was dimming. "Your dad felt sorry for me because I could barely walk. But what he didn't know is that it was all a ruse. When I left this place at night, I would hire a driver to take me to a private gym across the river. I trained like an Olympian, conditioning my mind and body for this..." She coughed again. "This final dress."

"You still haven't said, why," Shawna said softly. "Why kill everyone? Just to satisfy your revenge?"

The light in Candace's dark eyes began to fade. "Not only that."

"Then why?" Standing in the blanching daylight after a night she had barely survived, Shawna needed to know everything.

"Because your father and I were working toward the same goal, even if he didn't know it."

"I still don't understand," said Shawna.

"I wanted this place to close as much as he did." Candace lifted a trembling finger and pointed it accusingly at Bill. "I tried to plunge it into financial ruin, but Ron was onto me and squelched every attempt I made to bankrupt the theater. I blackmailed him so he couldn't fire me. He and Dougal had been running their small-time drug operation out of this place for years. Fixing that fuse box to kill Dougal was easy. I thought that was enough to bring this place down, but I was wrong."

"But you couldn't have acted alone," Shawna said. "Who helped you?"

"Ron, was more than happy to help with my plan at first. He thought it was a prank and, sadist that he was, he enjoyed terrifying you. He was the one who chased you around the basement the first time, not Penny, but he didn't know the extent of my full plan. Once he found out and he tried to stop me," Candace made a hideous noise as she mimed slashing her own throat.

"So," she continued. "I played the long game for only one reason."

"And what reason is that, pray tell?" asked Bill bitterly.

Candace's eyes softened as they gazed up at Bill. "I thought once everyone was dead, including your daughter, and I was the lone survivor, you would reach out to me as the only one who would truly understand. Then, when this place was torn down and your dream development was built, you could retire as Mayor, and we could live off the wealth, be together, forever, happy..." Her words faded and her eyes glazed over.

Bill folded like a sack and collapsed against the side of his car. "Did she say she killed everyone?"

Shawna nodded. Then she remembered Rex and Katie. There could be other survivors as well. "Dad, use the radio, please!"

"I'm on it."

Bill jumped to make the call while Shawna watched, with suspended horror and sadness, as the life slowly drained from Candace Laherty. By the time help arrived, Candace was gone--her broken soul was floating somewhere in the ether, and Shawna had forgiven her Dad--for everything.

Dale Cartwright arrived with the police and ambulances, ready to write the story that would propel the young journalist to national renown.

∼

REX DID SURVIVE Booth's bullet. And Katie, and the other members of the chorus, were found safe but terrified in the trap room beneath the stage. RJ's body was discovered center stage beneath a single bright spotlight. He died with a smile on his face, having achieved at least one of his goals.

The horrific events at Tullytown Players made national

news. Mayor Bill stayed to face the storm. Shawna offered to face it with him, but Bill insisted on sending her away for an extended vacation in Europe. During her six-month trek across several countries, Shawna made many friends--including a French graduate student with whom she had her first real love affair. She also learned about the world and reached a decision about her future.

When she returned home, the news had died down, the old barn had been razed to its foundation stones, and Bill retired from his position to dedicate himself to his new real estate venture.

While they were driving down the highway, they passed the now empty lot where the majestic old barn had once stood. It was winter now. The bare branches of the willow tree bent forlornly over the dim grass. Bulldozers were lined up, ready to turn the soil for the new development. Shawna asked her Dad why, with all the heat he had taken in the wake of what had come to be known as the Tullytown Terror, he had decided to stay.

"I guess I'm just a small-town boy at heart," Bill said. "But not you." He reached over and patted Shawna's hand. "Did you find the apartment you wanted?"

"Yup," Shawna said, gazing out at the pleasing winter landscape as it rushed by the car window. "It's only a studio, but it's close to all the theaters. And I've been chatting with a few agents online."

Bill took a deep breath and said, "Well, honey. Good luck."

"You mean 'break a leg', Dad."

They both laughed as they turned down the lane toward Pennbrook Farms. It was to be their last home-cooked meal together for a while.

# Final Dress

# AFTERWORD

Of the many amusing lines in the Hollywood classic *All About Eve*, my favorite has to be when Eve attempts to help Broadway star Margot Channing with her wardrobe backstage. Margot's wisecracking assistant Birdie, brilliantly played by Thelma Ritter, warns her to leave it alone, quipping, "...next to a tenor, a wardrobe woman is in the touchiest thing in show business." Ha! So true.

Although some of the characters in this story are fictional composites of real-life individuals I've known during my many years of working in the theater—exaggerated for dramatic effect, of course—there really is a Judith.

The original Judith goes back many years, and stories about her have achieved, through word of mouth, a certain notoriety among wardrobe staff in productions ranging from Broadway to the provinces. It's become such an inside joke that the name "Judith" has evolved into other parts of speech. For example, "Who Judithed that zipper?" or "Does this hem look too Judithy?" or "That outfit's so Judith."

Who says a person working behind the scenes can't

achieve the same fame as its most dazzling stars? I hope I did Judith proud.

This was a fun book to write, and if you enjoyed your time here, please leave a review on Amazon and Good-Reads. It's the bread and butter of the indie publisher, so please, even a good rating helps. If you're a fan of campy old-school horror, I have all kinds of goodies for you to check out on the following pages.

Thanks for reading Final Dress, and goodnight!

XOXO

Regina Saint Claire

**ABOUT THE AUTHOR**

Regina writes adult and young adult fiction, but always with a dark flair. Writing honors include a Watty Award for best horror novel and multiple screenwriting awards, including a Webby Honoree. Regina is co-editor of the popular Book Worms Horror Zine and co-hosts the Right Brain Café podcast.

Find Regina, and her alter-ego Batilda, at her BookTube channel, Regina's Haunted Library, and on her blog RSaint-Claire.com.

# R. Saint Claire

# The Starlet Suite

# THE STARLET SUITE
ORIGINALLY PUBLISHED IN WE'RE NOT HOME ANTHOLOGY

"Hollywood and Vine," I announced, sliding into the sticky back seat of the cab parked outside LAX.

I was hoping my words sounded cool, as if I knew it was a cliché. Plucky, off-handed irony with a geeky fascination for Old Hollywood horror, not to mention country gal flair, was my *brand* after all. I owed it to my 500K Instagram followers to keep up appearances. But the cabbie, Bernie from his license on display near the meter, appeared unimpressed. I shifted my gaze from his dark-ringed eyes in the cab's rearview mirror's reflection to the crease in the back of his neck.

"Hotel Paradiso," I said, clearing my throat. "It's a big old dinosaur of a hotel-"

"I know it," he said gruffly and with a slight laugh. He switched on the meter and pulled into traffic. We trundled slowly along, passing cars, concrete, and the occasional palm tree. I'd seen the bird's eye view of the LA freeway so many times in movies. Now I imagined myself from that angle, a fresh new face with stars in her eyes, poised on the knife's edge of fame. What would her future hold? Lost in my Hollywood dream, I almost forgot to document the moment in a post.

I pulled out my phone. I had lost all but one bar during the flight from Bristol (Tennessee, that is) but I'd be able to juice up again as soon as I reached my hotel. I had found the Hotel Paradiso at LADDITIES.com and booked it for its downtown location, kitschy ambience--located on the same block as the original Brown Derby--and its reputation for being haunted.

Putting myself in "scary" situations and getting out of them by the seat of my Daisy Dukes is also part of my brand. My followers love me! So much so that in just a few months, if everything goes as planned, I'll be able to quit my day job as a checkout girl at the Winn-Dixie—cheeky irony aside, I hate that job!--and support myself solely from my influencer "career." I'm putting career in quotes because I still can't quite believe it. Neither can my mom who nearly lost her mind when I dropped out of the dental assistant program where I had a "good future" and the chance to meet a "cute dentist."

"But you're twenty-one now," she told me, "and I can't stop you from living your life."

Speaking of living, I wanted to catch every moment of my trip so I twisted in my seat to snap a quick selfie with the cab driver in the background. I made the appropriate expression, open-mouthed, striking just the right notes of apprehension and excitement. I even caught ole Bernie shooting me a cold glare in the rearview. Pleased with my composition, I then went about posting the image on Instagram, adding a few OMG gifs and an animated arrow pointing at Bernie's cold, empty eyes with the words "my first friend in LA" in bleeding Frankenstein font. I hit "post" and then settled back in the seat and waited for the cascade of "likes" and heart emojis to pour in.

When we turned off Rodeo onto Sunset Boulevard, I rested my phone on the edge of the open cab window and pointed it at the sky to capture the towering palm trees floating by. Corny, I know, but that shot was *de rigueur* for any Hollywood story.

I was giggling at some of the first comments my post inspired when I realized Bernie had asked me a question. I leaned over the seat and with my best Southern manners asked, "Pardon me?" My nose twitched at the musky Playboy air freshener swinging from the rearview.

"I said how long you staying at the, uh, Hotel Paradiso?" His tongue ran over the name of my hotel like he was sealing a joint. "Or ya just renting by the hour?"

I was silent for several beats before I understood the meaning of his disgusting joke. Flushing to the roots of my highlighted hair, I sat back in the seat, feeling suddenly nauseous from the seesaw bounce of the car and Bernie's ugly laugh.

*Fuck that dude!*

I couldn't get out of the cab fast enough when he swung up to the corner.

"Hollywood and Vine!" he cried out like an old talkie director yelling "cut" through a megaphone. "Or would you prefer I drive you to the hotel?" His gruff voice rumbled with sarcasm as he pointed a thick finger up the block.

"This is fine," I barked, opening the back door with a huff.

"Keep the change," I said, floating a ten-dollar bill through the slot. I didn't want to feel his greasy fingers brushing mine. I hopped out of the cab with as much dignity as I could muster.

*Some men are just pigs*, I thought, straightening my denim skirt that had hiked up during the ride so that the faux button rivets made a straight line from belly button to crotch. I slammed the cab door shut. Then, with sudden horror, I realized I'd forgotten my duffle bag.

I ran after the cab screaming, "Hey!"

Bernie braked at the light, and I had to suffer the humiliation of knocking on his side window. The look he gave me was the epitome of gross, like he thought I was making a date with him or something, until he comprehended my sign language and popped the back door lock. I retrieved my bag with a shudder of disgust, kicked the door shut, and coughed up a mouthful of exhaust fumes as Bernie's cab was absorbed into the oblivion of traffic. I dragged my bag onto the concrete sidewalk, regretting not capturing the entire exchange in a live broadcast.

I took a deep breath and looked around. Capitol Records' iconic stack of 45s hovered high on the hill above me. In front of me stretched the famous Hollywood Walk of Fame.

Story One, Bernie the sleaze-bag cab driver leads into Story Two, welcome to the Hotel Paradiso!

As my white cowboy boots stamped the sidewalk, stopping occasionally to take in the stars' names embedded in the dirty concrete, I found myself humming the Eagles' *Hotel California* guitar solo--blond bushy-haired Joe Walsh was the one player, couldn't remember the other guy's name. Stevie Nicks said Walsh was the love of her life. Not Lindsey? Weird.

I was so absorbed in the music ringing in my head, and chasing the stars down the boulevard, that I passed the hotel and had to backtrack half a block.

When I reached 333 Hollywood Boulevard, I stopped in

my tracks, mouth agape, and gazed at the mammoth hotel towering above me like the gates King Kong crashed through. The façade boasted a Caribbean motif evident in the palm frond cornices and the carved letters above the door spelling out PARADISO in a font worthy of a *South Pacific* movie poster. The cornerstone read 1925. That was a long time ago, before my great-great-grandmother was born. Now I was humming a Beatles' tune.

More of my weird vintage quirky shit was flowing from my creative pores and I wasn't even recording.

I immediately rectified it by pulling my phone from my bag, rubbed off whatever grit remained of Bernie and his cab on my denim skirt, and pointed it at the hotel. Spreading my feet apart in place of a tripod, I took a shot starting from the gritty sidewalk and made a slow tilt to the roof. According to the website, the last two letters of the giant neon sign suspended from the upper floors hadn't lit up in decades, so that at night it spelled out only *Paradi*.

*A parody of my life?* I wondered with a jolt of apprehension. Just then, a black-clad, black-haired couple of indeterminable gender pushed through the revolving doors accompanied by a blast of stale AC.

I panned my screen to follow them as they sallied forth into the concrete haze.

"Too early for vampires," I uttered softly so only my camera phone could hear. The taller of the two turned to glance back and pop me the bird.

Hoping I'd caught all of that, I dropped my phone back in my purse, picked up my duffle bag, and hoisted it on my shoulder. I was ready to check into my room and relax before my big meeting later with a few brand reps.

A surge of excitement tingled my flesh as I passed through the revolving door into another world.

The lobby was even grander in scale and faded opulence than the website pictures depicted. Marble pillars shaped like palm trees supported a high ceiling painted to look like the night sky. Rimming the base from column to column was a mural. The faded paint depicted a monkey doing a one-arm hang from a branch and a lion poised on a rock, about to pounce on unsuspecting prey.

I was wondering if anyone had changed the light bulbs marking out the constellation of Scorpio when the hotel desk clerk greeted me with a formal "Good afternoon."

Again, I was sorry I'd put my phone away when I noticed the desk clerk was a dead ringer for Lloyd in *The Shining*. Reed thin in a red dinner jacket and shiny black hair parted like an arrow had split it down the middle, he stood stick-straight as if he'd been waiting there since time immemorial, his waxwork hands folded calmly on the high marble desk.

"Hi," I said, letting my bag slide to the floor. I hated that bag my mom loaned me, one of those hideous floral prints that did not fit in at all with my quirky vintage aesthetic. But I hadn't the time (or money) to get a new one when I'd received the message from an L.A. agent through my Twitter account, informing me they were interested in having me audition for a series of promotional videos and photos. If accepted, I'd earn more money in one weekend than in all my Winn-Dixie paychecks combined. Wardrobe, hair, and make-up would be provided, plus a designer "gift bag" of indeterminate value. Their website boasted models with Chanel bags so I was hopeful. All I had to do was provide my own transportation and lodging for three days. The audition would be an informal meet and greet party. **Just be yourself**, the message advised.

That's when I discovered the Hotel Paradiso's downtown location and cheap rates. The Paradiso's sordid history included several mob hits, fatal overdoses, and a suicide by a blond starlet named Janet Jennings in 1936 (or was she pushed?) Errol Flynn bedded a bobby-soxer somewhere in those hallowed halls making him the forties equivalent of being Me-Too'd, and the Black Dahlia herself, Elizabeth Short, had roomed here with several other girls before making her grim date with destiny. They say the wannabe starlet was still alive when her killer started sawing her in half, that she died from shock, that they found excrement in her stomach, which meant she'd been forced to-

"Thank you, Miss Reynolds, your room is on the fourteenth floor," said the Lloyd look-alike, real name Earl according to his gold nametag. He slid the metal key (no plastic cards in this joint) across the slick marble counter toward me.

"Call me Joni," I said.

His cold stare sent a chill from my dark roots to my Cuban heels.

Trying but failing to hold Earl's gaze, I attempted to lighten the mood by remarking that the fourteenth floor was actually the thirteenth floor.

"Come again?" Earl lifted his pointed chin and blinked rapidly.

"Hotels never have thirteen floors because of bad luck, right? So they skip it and go straight to fourteen, which still makes it the thirteenth floor."

Earl's hand shot out like a serpent's tongue and swiped back the key. "Perhaps you'll be more comfortable in 1925."

He slid a new key under my nose. "The starlet suite," he said.

I caught a flash of mockery in his dark gaze, but the

starlet suite sounded intriguing. A high floor would give me a great view of the city for photos.

"Cool." I took the key.

Through a tight, toothless smile, Earl uttered, "Have a pleasant stay."

I was going to ask him if I could take his picture for my Insta, perhaps one of me behind the desk wearing a bellhop cap askew on my head about to slam my hand down on the counter bell. But something about Earl's gaze stopped me cold. His eyes held the same hollowed out look as Bernie's, like he was dead inside. Maybe L.A. just does that to people.

*Losers!*

"Thanks," I said. Working my carefree swagger, I turned and headed for the elevators. My white cowboy boots slapped noisily against the marble floor. Happily, an elevator yawned open for me as I approached. I stepped inside and watched the doors do a slow wipe across Earl's dour waxwork face.

*Weirdo!*

During the slow, bumpy ride to the nineteenth floor, I stared at my reflection in the thumb-printed brass door. The lighting was far from flattering. I was too young for those deep circles under my eyes. I raked my hand through my limp hair, wondering if I had time for a blow-out before my audition. The elevator groaned and bounced as it reached the building's heights. The brass dial stopped at the number 19, and the door slid slowly open like a curtain parting to reveal a morbid tableau. The tastefully tawdry Old Hollywood glam of the lobby had given way to a seedy, dimly hit hallway with a vacuum cleaner abandoned beside a grimy window looking out on an airshaft. I stepped onto the gray carpeting which I could tell from the edges had once been beige. Water stains clung to the mottled wallpaper like lichen on a gravestone. A faded gold decal, peeling at the edges, pointed the way to my room.

The strap of my bag was digging a trench into my shoulder, otherwise, I would have pulled out my phone and done a tracking shot down the dark hallway, but I could do a pick-up later. Through flickering pools of fluorescent lights, I traversed the dismal winding hall, turning too many corners to count, until I reached my destination. I giggled when I saw that there was indeed a tiny placard with faded gold script announcing "The Starlet Suite."

*I will definitely get a shot of that.*

Already composing an Insta story in my head, I turned the key in the lock. My anticipation of art deco elegance was thwarted by the reality of a sad single bed shrouded with a navy blue quilt that had seen better days, next to it a night table with a cheap lamp, burn mark on the plastic shade. A tiny desk butted up against a wall painted a sad shade of beige. A chest of drawers sagged in one corner next to a small writing desk. I shook off the depressing image of me sitting at that desk writing postcards home.

*I'm only staying a few nights. This is rad!*

I dropped my bag and walked to the window to part the rubber-backed blue drapes. A puff of dust exploded in my face. I was about to head back to the lobby to demand of Earl better accommodations when I sucked in my breath at the incredible view.

A soft pink haze clung to rolling mountains in the distance and in between was the city itself. Ribbons of roads cut through sun-spangled high-rises. Everywhere there was movement and sound, a cacophony of car horns, impatient dreamers all trying to make their marks.

*Which is exactly why I'm here!*

I turned my back on the invigorating landscape,

releasing with a shoulder shrug any insecurities stirred by the cold reception of Bernie and Earl. They probably came to L.A. decades ago with big dreams and now they were bitter as hell.

*Not my problem!* I thought as I began to unpack.

An hour later, I lay on the bed with my phone plugged into the only outlet in the room and scrolled through my Insta feed.

My heart skipped a beat when a new message dinged in. Valerie Winn was checking in to make sure I'd arrived and to remind me that the meet and greet started at eight and that the dress was "creative and casual." My eyes scanned the shabby room to where the three outfits I had pulled together hung on a metal bar like outlaws on a gallows. I imagined the other influencers in attendance wearing designer clothes: YSL, Chanel, all the latest styles. I could only hope my "country girl in the big city" look of Daisy Dukes, checked shirt tied high beneath my boobs, and my short and sassy boots *made for walkin'* would do the trick. Maybe I'd buy myself a cheap straw cowboy hat from that Mexican shop I spotted driving in. I'd even stick a piece of straw in my mouth, like Axl Rose stepping off the bus in the *Welcome to the Jungle* video. That was my "brand" after all. That's what Valerie liked about me when she contacted me weeks ago.

**I'll be there!** I texted back with an OMG! emoji.

I waited, anxiously tapping my foot until I received the thumbs up in response. Then, suddenly exhausted from the stress of travel, I lay back on the hard mattress and shut my eyes. Even someone my age needed her beauty sleep was my last thought before I drifted off.

I was in the elevator shaft, my entire body wrapped around the cable like I was climbing the dreaded gym class rope. Except that I never could tackle that athletic task, and realizing as much in my dream, I began to slide down the cable. The coiled metal burned my palms and bare thighs, sliced into my flesh. I couldn't hold on. Sirens whined in the distance. Perhaps help was coming but it was too late. I was falling. Falling!

"Why are you in my bed?" A soft voice, high and feminine, cut through the fog of my nightmare.

"Huh?" My eyes popped open. I stared at the stained ceiling with the dusty fan blades slicing through the air. Drool trickled from the corner of my mouth.

"Did DeMille send you to spy on me?" The voice was less sweet now, more cutting, more-

*What the fuck!*

I couldn't move. Some unseen force pressed down on my legs, my shoulders. Panicked thoughts of sudden paralysis shot through my brain until I recalled this happened sometimes when I first woke up, especially from a deep nap.

*Just breathe.*

Imitating techniques I'd seen on yoga videos, I breathed deeply through my nostrils. But as my eyes adjusted to the dim light, I noticed with growing horror a shadowy figure perched on the foot of the bed.

"Do you work for Metro?"

The whispered breath was as cold as the slim fingers now spidering up my leg.

A rush of adrenaline shook off the sleep paralysis. My hands pawed desperately at the air, trying to gain the purchase to hurl myself from the bed, when fingers circled my wrists, tight and cold as a metal vise.

"I was told I didn't have to share a room with another girl! Look how small this bed is! Look!"

I did look, into the face floating over me, at the platinum

waves coiling around the pencil-thin brows, the lipsticked-mouth tied like a tight red bow.

"Please," I uttered.

"Just tell me who you are?" she insisted, fingers tightening.

"Joni," I rasped.

"Crawford!" She sat back in awe for a moment and I took the opportunity to leap from the bed. But in rushing for the door, I collided with the desk, the sharp corner striking my belly. Yellowed sheets of hotel stationery scattered like fall leaves as I stumbled backward. I grappled for the doorknob, but she was on me again. Her slim arms circled my waist as she shoved me back toward the bed. I could feel the silk of her negligee, smell the heady notes of her perfume--Jungle Gardenia maybe.

"Don't go!" she implored. "We can share the room. I need to talk to someone." A sob escaped her small red mouth like a bird from its cage. "I've been stuck in this lousy room for a week waiting for my damn agent to call. I haven't eaten for days."

Something in her voice touched me, a desperation I could relate to perhaps. If this was a dream, it was a damn realistic one.

*Wait a minute*, I told myself as I stopped struggling with this slender but deceptively strong young woman who felt very real indeed, very much of flesh and blood. Here was a genuine ghost in a haunted hotel.

*Christ! This was Insta gold!*
*What starlet could this possibly be?*

Then it hit me.

"Janet?"

"Yes," she whispered, her cold lips trembling against my cheeks.

*The STARLET SUITE*

"Janet Jennings?"

"You are from the studio!" a hopeful note rang in her voice. "When do they want me to report? Tell Mr. DeMille I'll play any role! I'm not picky. I just want to act. I just want to-"

"Hey Janet, can you let go please?"

"Huh?"

"You're strangling me a little."

Her thin arms relaxed, and I wiggled out of her grip.

"I'm so sorry, my dear." Her voice was softer now, dulcet and breathy. "I got a bit carried away, I'm afraid. You frightened me, is all."

She took a few steps toward the night table and flicked on the lamp.

The light from the tilted shade illuminated the Jean Harlow look-alike with platinum Marcel waves and a powdered white complexion accented with circles of rouge on high cheekbones. She clutched an ivory silk negligee around her waist. I studied her exquisite face, wondering why had she done it? Why had Janet Jennings taken a dive out the nineteenth-floor window?

*If I could just get this ghost on camera.*

"Janet? Do you mind if I film you?"

"What?" Her baby blues brightened. "Are we going on set now?"

I eyed the door in case this wasn't a dream after all and I had to make a run for it. "I was thinking right here. Just a quick video."

Janet looked confused.

Flush with inspiration, I quickly scanned the room.

"Over here," I said, placing my hands on her slim shoulders and guiding her toward the window. With the blazing

California sunset framing her slim silhouette, I arranged her against the tall window frame.

"Hold that pose!" I instructed, stepping back to quickly retrieve my phone from off the bed. "The lighting is perfect."

"But my hair!" Janet's hands fiddled anxiously with her bob.

"It looks great a little messed up."

Her wide eyes blinked with incredulity. Perhaps because she'd been a ghost trapped in this room without a soul to talk to for so long, years judging by the dust, Janet eased into my company like fingers into a jar of cold cream.

"Are you sure I look all right?" She relaxed her shoulders enough for her negligee to open, revealing the white curve of her breasts. The silk edge teased the dark outlines of her nipples.

I picked up my phone and hit the camera icon, half expecting her image to disappear on the screen. It would be a testament to a sudden onset of madness on my part. Joni Reynolds, @JoRecountrygal, went to L.A. and lost her mind.

*Happens all the time*, I thought, making small adjustments with my new photo app. Not only did Janet Jennings' face appear on my phone screen in sharp focus, the camera loved her.

"Wait!" Janet erupted excitedly. "They always use a fan at the studio. Here's a trick." She turned and with a grunt pushed open the window. A warm breeze scented with orange blossoms and gasoline fumes wafted in. She spun back, and the air lifted her hair so that a platinum curl fell seductively over one eye. I caught the moment in a few quick snaps.

"Janet, can you turn your face a bit to the side, please?"

"Like this?" she asked. The amber magic-hour light spilled in, highlighting the perfection of her profile.

I gasped as I snapped away.

"Everything all right?" she droned. Her nerves seemed to have disappeared once she was under the spell of the camera.

"Yes, you're stunning."

A smile twitched the corner of her lips. A seasoned model, she arched back her throat so that her hair fell, Garbo-like, against her shoulders.

"Wow. That's incredible."

I took several more snaps, making quick adjustments to the exposure until I found the right balance. The thousand promises glimmering in the cityscape reverberated in Janet's sultry blue gaze. She was Jean Harlow in the flesh! Perhaps, I thought, pausing to scroll through the photos, she was too much like Harlow. Hollywood hadn't needed another blonde bombshell. If she had only waited for the real Jean Harlow to die of renal failure at the tender age of twenty-six, she could have made it.

*Was fame that fickle? And what did that mean for me? Would there be another girl at the party tonight with highlighted hair, sporting the homespun cow-gal look?*

If so, I wanted to be the first one to make the right impression.

*What time is it anyway?*

"Joni, is everything all right? You seem distracted. Are the pictures okay?"

"The pictures are wonderful, Janet. It's just that I'm due at a party soon and-"

"A party?" Janet clapped her hands together like a little girl. Her eyes shimmered. "Where?"

"At the Ruba on Sunset. Know it?"

Janet shook her curls. "No, I haven't been to a party in so long." Her rinky-dink voice hit a sad note.

"I better get going," I said, mostly to myself. I was convinced that somehow I'd wake from the weird dream I was having.

*What were the lyrics from the Tom Waits song about motel rooms smelling like diesel? 'You take on the dreams of those who slept here.'*

"What's that you're looking at?" Suddenly Janet was beside me, her cool hand resting on my arm.

"Just uploading your photos. Hey! You already got a few likes and hearts."

"Likes and hearts?" she cooed, taking a closer look.

"You have fans, Janet."

"Really?"

Her gaze locked hungrily on mine. Suddenly, her closeness felt stifling. She was a cat climbing on top of me while I slept to siphon off my breath. I made a move to the bathroom, but she did a fast foxtrot to block me.

"Where are you going?" she asked.

I squirmed under the feathered softness of her cool breath.

"I need to take a shower before my party."

"Oh, that's right. The party." Her dimpled chin dropped.

I was about to navigate my route to the bathroom, knowing that when I emerged from a fresh shower that this ghost would be washed away like the remnants of Ivory soap down the drain, that the photos I uploaded to Insta would have vanished. But the phone in my hand continued to beep and ding its approbation.

Quick as a cougar, Janet snatched the phone from my hand.

"They love me!" she said, gazing down at the screen. She threw her head back. "I'm a star!"

"You certainly are," I replied indulgently. "Now if you don't mind, I—hey, that hurts."

Janet's hands, small, white, determined, were once again bracketing my wrists. "This is my big break!" she said. "And I need to grab it!"

Realizing she was steering me toward the open window, I tried to wrestle out of her grip, but she proved too strong. The soft kitten eyes had turned hard and feral.

"Janet, stop!" My bare feet dragged against the rough carpet as she hurled me across the room. I collapsed against the windowsill. Her robe opened, revealing small, but perky breasts. She struggled out of the negligee, tossing it aside as I regained my footing. Clad only in creased silk tap-pants, she lunged at me. I fought hard to fight her off. Choking on mouthfuls of her Jungle Gardenia perfume, I found myself weakening. With a swift swipe of her marabou-trimmed mules, she cut my legs out from under me.

"Bitch!" she cried, platinum locks coiling before her eyes. "I'll be damned if you're going to steal that part from me!"

"It's not a part, it's a party—I—"

Her nails, bright red and filed to sharp points, raked across my cheek. My hands flew instinctively to my face to ward off her blows. In the struggle I became twisted, and suddenly I found myself staring into the vortex of the L.A. sidewalk, nineteen stories down, Dutch-tilted and deadly. A wave of nausea rose from my belly, knocked me off-kilter. With windmilling arms, I made a desperate grab for the window frame, but Janet had anticipated that move. She wrenched my right wrist hard, and then her pearly white teeth bit down on my fingers. I screamed as the pain seared up my arm. Then, she released her bite, and like a trained gymnast, she gripped the window frame with both hands and mule-kicked into my chest, knocking the wind out of me with the soles of her size-fives.

I huffed, folded into the empty space behind me. The edges of the window frame grazed my fingertips and then I was falling, incomprehensibly at first, and then with growing horror as the windows zipped past me.

*Wake up! Wake up! This is all part of your dream! Wake up!*

But the rushing air stole my scream. And as the grimy sidewalk came closer with each desperate spin, my blurred vision flashed snippets of the ghosts inhabiting each room of the Hotel Paradiso. The gangster's gun fired, Errol Flynn in only his sock suspenders chased a naked girl around a bed, and the Black Dahlia absently munched on a hamburger as she stood by the window gazing dreamily at the fading California sunset.

The impact, black as a screen after the credits rolled, produced no pain, only awful regret, that I'd blown my big chance, and that now I was nothing. Nothing at all.

∽

Janet Jennings exited the elevator dressed in short Daisy Dukes that just grazed the creases in her pert buttocks and a red and white plaid shirt tied at the waist. Her platinum Marcel waves bounced with each wide stride of her white cowboy boots.

Earl let out a slow whistle as she approached the registration desk.

"Howdy, partner," Janet said, lifting an imaginary ten-gallon hat.

"Howdy," Earl said. He raised one eyebrow. "Going to a rodeo?"

Janet shrugged. "Nope. Party at the Ruba."

"Working girl hours, eh?"

She shrugged, swinging the room key on her index finger. "Beats swinging hash."

Earl pursed his lips and ran his dark gaze from her face to the curve of her breasts resting on the high desk. "Have fun."

"I'll try." She drummed her red nails on the desk. "Maybe we can have a nightcap later."

Earl leaned forward on his palms. "Sounds like a date."

Police sirens, distant at first, screamed through the hollow silence of the lobby.

Janet cocked an eyebrow toward the street. "Sounds like you got trouble, Earl."

The corners of his thin lips bowed into a crocodile smile. "Nothing you have to worry your pretty head about."

"You're aces, Earl." She threw him a seductive wink then turned, wiggling her ass a bit as she sashayed across the lobby.

"Never give up, doll face," Earl called after her.

Janet twirled her fingers in the air.

Earl smiled, his dark eyes shimmering like stars, as he watched her pass through the revolving doors into the red pulse of an ambulance just pulling up to the curb. A few bystanders took out their phones and snapped away at the broken body lying limp on the sidewalk in a pool of dark blood. Janet reveled in the flashing lights for a moment as she lit her cigarette. Then she pivoted away from the ghastly scene and disappeared into the warm Hollywood night.

# R. SAINT CLAIRE
# CARNI

# The Vampires are Running the Asylum

# CODE RED

## R. SAINT CLAIRE

BOOK WORMS
HORROR ZINE
Season of the Witch
in this issue...
Witches vs. Babies by
GRADY HENDRIX
Saucy Sprat by
CLAY MCLEOD CHAPMAN
SCAN ME

Printed in Great Britain
by Amazon